This man had a take-charge attitude that calmed Haley without a word being spoken.

Colonel Brett Stanton squatted to the boys' level, but didn't invade their space. His sensitivity loosened their grip on Haley's hands, as if they were willing to meet the big guy halfway. A neat trick, all told.

"You hungry, boys?"

"Yes." Todd nodded, emphatic.

"Starving." Tyler sent a bullish look Haley's way. "She drove all day."

The man appeared to weigh Tyler's words. "Traveling on a holiday can be tough." Deep hazel eyes held her attention for short seconds but long enough to make her heart trip faster. Beat harder. "Does she have a name?"

"Aunt Haley." Tyler said the words with more than a little distrust.

"She's pwetty." Todd leaned a little closer to the man now, too, following his brother's lead. "And I like her yellow hair."

"It's drop-dead gorgeous," the man agreed easily. He tossed that crooked smile up to Haley, winked at her and reached for the boys' hands. "You guys ready to have Thanksgiving dinner with us?"

Books by Ruth Logan Herne

Love Inspired

Winter's End
Waiting Out the Storm
Made to Order Family
*Reunited Hearts
*Small-Town Hearts
*Mended Hearts
*Yuletide Hearts
*A Family to Cherish
*His Mistletoe Family

*Men of Allegany County

RUTH LOGAN HERNE

Born into poverty, Ruth puts great stock in one of her favorite Ben Franklinisms: "Having been poor is no shame. Being ashamed of it is." With God-given appreciation for the amazing opportunities abounding in our land, Ruth finds simple gifts in the everyday blessings of smudge-faced small children, bright flowers, freshly baked goods, good friends, family, puppies and higher education. She believes a good woman should never fear dirt, snakes or spiders, all of which like to infest her aged farmhouse, necessitating a good pair of tongs for extracting the snakes, a flat-bottomed shoe for the spiders, and for the dirt…

Simply put, she's learned that some things aren't worth fretting about! If you laugh in the face of dust and love to talk about God, men, romance, great shoes and wonderful food, feel free to contact Ruth through her website at www.ruthloganherne.com.

His Mistletoe Family
Ruth Logan Herne

Love Inspired

Recycling programs
for this product may
not exist in your area.

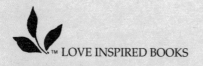 ™ LOVE INSPIRED BOOKS

ISBN-13: 978-0-373-81663-7

HIS MISTLETOE FAMILY

www.LoveInspiredBooks.com

Printed in U.S.A.

These things I have spoken unto you,
that in me ye might have peace.
In the world ye shall have tribulation: but be of
good cheer; I have overcome the world.
—*John* 16:33

This book is dedicated to LuAnn and Charlie Koch, dear friends who shared so much with so many. God certainly blessed me when he put you guys in my life over thirty years ago. Your love for God and Allegany County fed mine.

And to Melissa Endlich, whose ongoing advice, humor and guidance blesses each and every book I write, even though the image of a non-coffee-drinking NYC editor just seems wrong. So wrong!

Acknowledgments

First to LuAnn and Charlie for the stories they shared. To Dana Guinnip of Angelica, New York, for his advice on firefighting, chicken and biscuits and where to stage an accident scene.
To The Seekers (www.seekerville.blogspot.com) for their constant support and encouragement. You guys keep me laughing and grounded. To Tina and Mary for road-tripping with me when so few dare!
To Deb Giusti for always answering my military questions and never acting tired. To Homer Marple for establishing the Craft and Antique Co-op. His vision inspired "Bennington Station." To Vince, who is never afraid to challenge me, and I love a good challenge. To Beth and Mandy for their continued hands-on help with little things that make me look way smoother than I am. And my family, who continue to believe that following your dream is the best way to go. I couldn't agree more. Thank you for the daily encouragement, the hugs, the grins and the book sales. You guys mean the world to me.

Chapter One

Despair should never be allowed to rule Thanksgiving Day.

Haley Jennings eyed the two camouflage-clad little boys in her backseat, mentally searching for anything she might have ever learned about children in her twenty-eight years on the planet.

She came up empty. That didn't sound promising for the orphaned nephews now in her care.

Tear tracks snaked a path down three-year-old Todd's round cheeks, a worn, black stuffed kitty named Panther clutched tight against his chest. Five-year-old Tyler slumped against the corner of the car, burrowing, as if hoping to disappear into the upholstery. He shed no tears, but the quiet look of abandonment seemed worse for lack of emotion.

Scared. Uncertain. Handed off as though they were parcel post packages from one place to another. And no doubt hungry, but few restaurants were open this late on Thanksgiving Day, a should-be-glorious holiday of roast turkey, mashed potatoes, gravy and stuffing.

The thought of homemade stuffing made her mouth water. How much more must two little fellows be longing for a good old-fashioned holiday?

Part of her was glad their maternal great-aunt had found Anthony's will that named her the boys' guardian. Another part longed to run screaming.

She took the turn toward Jamison, knowing she had no food in her recently acquired no-frills apartment and the grocery store had closed mid-afternoon. And with the boys' meager belongings piled and shoved into every corner of her convertible, she had no room for a shopping trip and precious few funds to bankroll extra groceries this week.

Whoever said God's timing was perfect should be chastised, because this situation was about as far from perfect as life could get.

A flashing sign caught her attention as she approached the Park Round, the picturesque town circle surrounded by five country churches and a couple of pastors' homes.

Free Thanksgiving Dinner!
Join us from 2:00 till 5:00
on Thanksgiving Day
for a friend-filled holiday feast!
All are welcome!

An arrow pointed toward the back of Good Shepherd Church. An upgraded older building stood there, caught in the trees, an aged steeple rising white against the late-November drab of damp bark. A chill wind bowed the sticklike trees, but the white-washed hall was surrounded by cars and bathed in light from garden stake lamps below.

Dinner.

Free.

One glance at her dashboard clock said they were nearing the late side of the offer. She faltered, not wanting to subject the boys to any more disappointments on a day that should be filled with family. Fun. Food. Rejoicing.

The word *feast* turned her hands on the wheel. Or maybe it was the Holy Spirit. In any case, she angled the car up the drive and into a parking spot. She climbed out and tilted the driver's seat forward, banging her head and knee in the process.

Red ragtops weren't designed as family vehicles.

"Where are we going?" Tyler eyed her from his booster seat, glancing around to discern an easy way out of the car. There wasn't one.

"Climb out this way." Haley jerked her head toward her side as she struggled with the puzzlelike latches on Todd's car seat. Who knew you needed a math degree to figure out a five-point latch system? "Once I've got your brother out, that is."

As she pulled Todd from the backseat, she managed to bump his head, too. Not too badly, but enough to start the waterworks flowing, full steam ahead. "Oh, baby, I'm sorry." She crooned the words and rubbed the spot, wishing she'd thought to cushion his head with her hand while extracting him.

Next time, for sure.

"I hate this car." Tyler made the pronouncement as he finagled his way across small bags and totes shoved into the backseat.

"I'm not all that fond of it myself at this moment," Haley assured him. "But it's paid for and it runs and at one time it was a status symbol. Cute blonde chick in blazing hot red convertible with mag wheels."

"It's dumb." Tyler brushed off his five-year-old knees with an air of impatience. "And we don't fit."

There lay the crux of the problem. Todd and Tyler hadn't "fit" in a long time. These two little boys had lost their mother and father in the past two years and they'd been shuffled around to various homes for months—way too much change for a level-headed grown-up.

Two boys, aged three and five?

Ridiculous.

But possibly made more outlandish by her half brother's will naming her their legal guardian. Anthony scarcely knew her. She barely knew him. They shared a father and a legal relationship recognized by courts. Other than that? They'd met half a dozen times over the years, mostly at weddings and funerals.

What was he thinking?

The door to the hall swung open and a couple of old-timers stepped out. "Ma'am, may I hold the door for you?" An old man dipped his head in courtly fashion, a shock of white hair dancing in the wind. "That wind's a breath-stealer, sure enough."

She hesitated, not wanting to ask if there was still food, not daring to get the boys' hopes up only to dash them again. "I, um…"

"Plenty of good eats in there, miss, and I think those two boys are just the thing for them folks inside. Nothin' like bein' 'round a couple o' young-uns to remind us why we keep on keepin' on."

His words eased her path. Did he see the hunger? Or the fear? Or both?

In any case, Haley grasped a boy's hand in each of hers and walked the last twenty paces. "Thank you, sir."

"Jed, have a mind, will you, and close that door," bossed a woman's voice from within. "My tablecloths are being tugged every which way!"

The old guy exchanged a grin with Haley, winked at the boys and hollered back, "Customers, mother! We've got two young soldiers in need of a bite."

Haley stepped inside, Todd on her right, Tyler on her left. Silence descended as she and the boys moved from the front room into the gathering area, as if few in the room imagined little boys coming to Thanksgiving dinner at the church hall.

A tall man stepped forward. Fortyish. Good-looking. Square-shouldered. Broad-built. Dark hazel eyes matched military-cut hair, walnut-toned with hints of light. His assessing gaze went liquid brown while he pondered the boys at her side, as if recognizing something perfect and precious. He blinked and the look was gone, but the integral air of quiet authority and respect remained. Haley had the oddest urge to salute the big guy. Or maybe just hug him. Right about now, she could use a hug.

A pleased murmur stirred an air of delight through the room.

"Look at them!"

"Aren't they marvelous?"

"Oh, they are!"

"Who are they?"

"Oh, it doesn't matter. It's just so nice to see such handsome little boys at our feast!"

A tiny smile quirked the man's left cheek, just enough to show amusement tempered with respect, book-end qualities that few men in Haley's age range possessed.

This man had both and more, his take-charge attitude calming the confusion within her without speaking a word. He squatted to the boys' level, but didn't invade their space. His sensitivity loosened their grip on Haley's hands, her arms, as if willing to meet the big guy halfway. A neat trick, all told.

"You hungry, boys?"

"Yes." Todd nodded, emphatic.

"Starving." Tyler sent a bullish look Haley's way. "She drove all day and didn't want to stop anyplace."

"Ah." The man appeared to weigh Tyler's words.

"Traveling on a holiday can be tough. Stores close early. Some restaurants don't open at all."

"Really?" Tyler poked his head closer to the man, then hooked a thumb back to Haley. "That's what *she* said, but I figured she was making it up."

The man's gaze traveled up, and not all that quickly, as if appreciating the journey. Deep hazel eyes locked and held her attention long enough to make her heart trip faster. "Does *she* have a name?"

"Aunt Haley." Tyler said the words with more than a little distrust.

"She's pwetty." Todd leaned closer to the man, too, following his brother's lead. "And I like her yellow hair."

"It's drop-dead gorgeous," the man agreed easily. He spiked that crooked smile up to Haley and had no idea what his gentle manner was doing to her. He winked at her, stood, reached for the boys' hands, and to Haley's surprise, they moved forward. "You guys ready to have Thanksgiving dinner with us?"

"Yes!"

"I am." Tyler nodded, firm, obviously trying to contain his excitement. His reaction told Haley he was accustomed to disappointment. Her heart broke because she knew that feeling all too well.

"Haley? Haley, is that you?"

The little woman who helped run the mom-and-pop convenience store at the interstate junction bustled out from the kitchen and hurried their way. She flapped her apron and grinned, her high-wattage smile enough to make everything seem almost all right. "LuAnn."

"And Charlie's here, too," the older woman fussed, her silver hair dancing sparks from the fluorescent lights above. "He's going to be so excited to see you, dear, but who are your friends?" LuAnn Simmons bent low and stuck out a hand, but Haley noticed she handled the boys with deference, like the man had done, hanging back, not encroaching their space.

"My nephews," Haley explained.

The man palmed Tyler's head in a sweet gesture, but he moved back as LuAnn stormed in. He didn't smile but his eyes grazed Haley, LuAnn and the boys. He dipped his chin slightly, noting the white-haired woman. "You're in good hands. No one goes hungry with Charlie and LuAnn around."

Haley knew that. She was a constant customer at their little store, its proximity to her new business venture making the Crossroads Mini-Mart a perfect spot for quick food. Consumed with building a new shopping cooperative just across the road, quick and easy food had become a mainstay in her life.

LuAnn's head bobbed, excited. "'When I was hungry, you gave me to eat. When I was thirsty, you gave me to drink.'"

The man's face darkened as if a shade had been pulled. He moved back to the kitchen area while LuAnn steered the boys to the still-laden buffet.

Todd cringed back, hesitating, but his nose twitched

as if the smell of food broke an unseen barrier. "This is Todd, LuAnn."

"Todd." He didn't take LuAnn's hand and she didn't force the issue. She sent him a bright smile, and her cheerful brown eyes made Haley feel less worried and alone. Amazing what a smile can do.

And a half smile, she noted as the tall man rejoined volunteers in the kitchen preparation area.

"And this is Tyler. He's five."

Tyler extended his hand to LuAnn. Haley sent him a smile of encouragement. "Thank you, Tyler. LuAnn is my friend. She and I work at stores near each other."

"Oh." Tyler tried to look polite, then failed as his eyes darted to the buffet table. "Can we eat now?"

"You most certainly can." LuAnn drew him forward. She picked up a sturdy stoneware plate and waved a hand. "I know you're big enough to pick out your own food, Tyler, but this table's a little high. I think if I hold your plate and you tell me every little thing you want on it, we'd make a good team. What do you say?" She angled a birdlike glance his way. "May I be your partner?"

"Yes, ma'am."

Haley owed the older woman for handling Tyler so easily. She wouldn't have had a clue. She followed LuAnn's example, showing Todd the food, letting him choose as he held the black cat snug beneath his arm, unconcerned when he wanted twelve black olives because LuAnn hadn't protested when Tyler asked for extra gherkins and stuffing. By the time they got the boy's meat cut and grace said, LuAnn took a place alongside the boys and between a dozen gathered folks and waved Haley away. "Go. Fill your plate. I've got this covered." She flashed a smile at the boys, watching as Todd struggled with the height of the table and the plate.

"Try this, LuAnn."

The warm rumble of the man's voice pulled Haley's attention away from food. She would have thought that feat impossible at the moment, but something in that tone…

With one arm he hiked Todd up, then slipped a thick old-time phone book beneath Todd's bottom. He re-settled Todd onto his new raised "seat," and the better vantage point made the little boy shine with delight. He peeked up at the man and offered a dimpled grin and a quick salute.

The man's smile faded.

Pain stilled his jaw. Shadowed his eyes.

LuAnn sent him a motherly look of concern, but said nothing.

He stepped back, turned and moved off to the kitchen again, *in* the crowd but not *of* it, Haley was sure on that.

LuAnn shoulder-nudged Haley's leg. "You. Food. Go."

Haley filled her plate, the scents and sounds of a family Thanksgiving surrounding her, a big-screen TV perched on a table at the far end of the hall covering the day's football offerings while people gathered at tables eating, chatting, laughing.

If she'd wished for a perfect Thanksgiving, this would be it.

The fact that this was as close to family as she could possibly get just made that admission more sad.

Pretty yellow hair?

And then some, thought Colonel Brett Stanton as he commandeered cleanup in the hall kitchen, the image of Haley's long, curly blond hair worth remembering.

He shouldered his way through a nest of female busybodies who'd gathered out of sight to wonder about the blonde and the two boys.

Brett didn't wonder. He knew. He'd seen the longing right off. The hunger. The fear and uncertainty clouding their day. He might not know their story, but he knew the wistful look of wanting, wishing, hoping to have or be a family.

Sadness gripped from within, a clear-cut knife strike, the mistakes of the past wrangling a grip on the future.

"Aren't they darling?" LuAnn hurried up beside him, two plates in hand. She handed them off to one of the chatterbox women and grasped Brett's arm. "Thank you for being so nice to them. I'm sure Haley's a little overwhelmed at the moment—"

Brett would have gone straight to shell shock, but he let the understatement pass.

"And this couldn't happen at a worse time…"

Five sets of ears attempted nonchalance as they keened closer like covert agents on an info-gathering mission.

"But I know she'll be fine. Just fine. And I'm so glad she saw our sign flashing out front. That's what drew them in, you know." LuAnn gave his arm a quick hug. "Brett, thank you for letting us use the sign today."

She bustled back out, leaving the women and Brett to fill in the blanks. He finished scrubbing the second big roaster and handed it off to Kate McGee for drying. The elderly woman accepted it and offered, "I don't know about the rest of you, but it did my heart good to see that little crew come walking in, all tired and bedraggled."

"Ah. A Kate-ism looms, no doubt." Maude McGinnity flashed Brett a grin he couldn't help but return.

"Maude, you felt it, too," Kate insisted. "I saw it in your face, you old bird. You got all moony and goofy the minute you laid eyes on them boys."

"I did not."

"Did, too, and I know why," Kate continued. "They were travelers, finding their way home. Needing food. Lodging. So nice and Christmassy."

"Oh, my land." Maude shook her head, shooed the three less-productive women out of the kitchen and made a skeptical face as she layered pots and pans in the kitchen cupboards just so. "You do go on, Kate. Whereas I'd have said they're hungry, most places are closed and we were mighty handy. What do you say, Brett?"

Brett didn't make it through twenty-five years of this man's army by being slow on the take. Uh-uh. He knew these women, knew they'd been watching his initial exchange with the blonde and the boys and there was no getting by the hawkeyes of the Jamison Hose Company's Ladies' Auxiliary.

Time to employ diversionary tactics and pretend the waiflike family hadn't affected him. "The little guy's about the same age as your great-grandson, isn't he, Kate?"

"Looks to be."

"How's Aiden doing?"

"Adorable! Just adorable!" Kate's face broadened with laughter, family pride deepening each and every wrinkle in her sweet, old face.

Maude sent Brett a look, half-grudging, half-complimentary, recognizing his ploy. He returned it with a wink, unstoppered the deep commercial-sized sink and moved to the back door. "I'm going to check cleanup outside before it gets too dark."

"Thank you, Brett."

He tipped the sludge-green brim of his army cap her way before stepping through the back door.

Bleak November greeted him. Dank. Dark. Gloomy. Gray. Fall had been vibrant with color, but the leaves were pretty much gone now. Here and there a larch tree stood in golden splendor, painting points of light along the Allegany hillsides, their amber needles lingering until late in the season.

November. A month of remembrance for so many. Veteran's Day… Thanksgiving…

The chilly, dull days afforded too much thinking time, Brett determined. The late-autumn month offered too many moments to bow his head and wish he'd done things differently. But it was too late now.

"Brett, you need help out here?" Charlie Simmons ambled his way, a snug knit cap covering his balding head. LuAnn's touch, for sure. "Kate said you were looking to make sure nothing got left undone."

God bless Kate McGee because they all knew he was more likely escaping too many people. Too much interaction. Too much of a good thing that slipped, quicksilver, through his hands. "Just figured I'd catch a breath and give the women some space in the kitchen."

"I hear ya." Charlie flashed him a knowing smile before he settled his gaze along the now-diminished row of cars in the parking lot. "We did good today."

Charlie's comment embraced more than food. He meant they'd opened doors for folks who might never take a handout, but a party, sponsored by the local firemen and their wives?

That took the sting out of neediness and put it in a whole new light.

When I was hungry, you gave me to eat…

Brett had done that often while deployed. He'd fed locals, helped the downtrodden, guided the weary, all while wearing the uniform of the country he loved.

But he'd paid a price he'd never considered, and that realization bit to the core of his being. If only... His wandering thoughts ground to a halt when a warm voice drew his attention to the entrance door.

The blonde...

Haley, he corrected himself internally.

Stepped through the door, her generous smile a flash of sun in a time of rain. The boys followed, their faces more relaxed and somewhat sleepy.

"Haley!" LuAnn followed with Maude McGinnity. Both women bore bags of covered food dishes, the aluminum foil squeaking protest as they moved. "We need a home for some of these leftovers and you and the boys are just the ticket!"

Just the ticket?

The Mayberry-type saying fit the day, the occasion, the people and Jamison, New York, the picturesque little town nestled in the heart of Allegany County.

Haley turned. Surprise and pleasure brightened her profile. She didn't wave off the food or pretend not to need it. She helped LuAnn snug the packaged plates between tightly wedged items in the sporty red car, then hugged both women while the boys attempted to fasten their belts.

"Thank you." She smiled at Maude, then LuAnn, grasping each woman's hand in hers. "You have no idea how necessary this is right now. I had to use all my ready cash on last week's deliveries, the bank hasn't released the next draft on the loan as yet, and we need to have that final wing open next week."

"I know." LuAnn leaned forward, obviously understanding the woman's thread of conversation while Brett drew a complete blank. "And if you need anything, anything at all…"

"A babysitter." Haley lowered her voice and kept a grip on both women's hands. "This unexpected development has me in a crunch. Tomorrow is Black Friday and my retailers expect me on site. My cousin Alyssa hooked me up with Rory Madigan—"

"A lovely girl." Maude nodded approval. LuAnn's quick blink agreed.

"But she's an Irish dancer and has a feis this weekend in Buffalo. So I can use her tomorrow, but then there's Saturday and Sunday that need coverage."

"On a holiday weekend, to boot," LuAnn added, concerned.

"And our Jessie is due to deliver any minute," Charlie put in, "or we'd be glad to help out."

Brett stayed still. Silent. He hadn't meant to be part of this conversation and had every intention of ignoring his conscience. He'd spent the last two years living life alone. Quiet. In the background except for when it came to the fire department. Just him, the dog and an amazing room full of model trains.

He loved his volunteer firefighting job. Helping others. Battling fires. Covering inspections, as needed. Maybe he was always meant to be a battler and that's why the army had fit so well.

Too well.

"We'll figure it out," LuAnn promised as Haley

redirected Todd's fingers to engage his car seat straps. A tiny "click" said they got it done. "You take the boys home, get them settled and I'll see what I can come up with tomorrow. Okay?"

"God bless you, LuAnn." Haley hugged the older woman, her crush of blond hair reflecting the dawn-to-dusk light. She slid into the car, waved goodbye, backed out of the parking spot with ease and aimed the car toward the interstate and Brett's retirement-funded convenience store, but she raised a sweet hand as she made the corner turn, and her face—

Oh, that face—

Sent them a bright smile as if certain everything would work out in the end.

Brett only wished her youthful optimism held true. And just as dark thoughts seemed determine to resettle, a small, wriggling body stretched up in her backseat, peering out. The scrunched face caught Brett's gaze through the darkened rear window. The little fellow relaxed into a wide grin. The corner light gave just enough gleam for Brett to recognize Todd's features, his rounded eyes, cheeks and chin holding a hint of the baby he'd been not long ago, and the precocious preschooler he was now.

He waved at Brett. Just Brett. And somehow that tiny action, unprovoked, innocent and childlike, shoved those old thoughts aside. Way aside.

Brett smiled. Raised his hand.

The boy did the same, and in that moment Brett felt

a gnarly old door tug open. It was his heart, rusted and worn, struggling to work free.

And it felt good.

Chapter Two

"Boss? You're good?"

Brett nodded toward Steve Huber and Ramir Martinez, his two college-aged employees who got him through a crazy busy Black Friday at the Crossroads Mini-Mart. "Yes. See you guys tomorrow. And thank you." He met each young man's look with a smile of appreciation as he cleaned the narrow delicatessen area. "I don't know what I would have done without you today."

Steve grinned and Ramir offered a thumbs-up as they left. The young men came through in a pinch when Charlie and LuAnn's daughter decided to give birth mid-morning. And with the new shopping enterprise recently opened across the street?

The Crossroads had set record sales figures today. And that was nothing to take lightly in tough economic times.

Brett had pretty much decided he hated the idea of destination shopping when the fancy merchants' co-operative began stringing twinkle lights ad nauseam two weeks ago. But when their Black Friday business spilled over to his dolled-up convenience store directly across the two-lane road leading to I-86, he realized he might owe the developer an apology. And a thank you. Except for being a little short on workers, it had been an amazing day. And he'd felt good about being out here. Manning the store. Making special-order fast food along the deli wall.

He'd do a repeat performance tomorrow because Les Simmons, Charlie's brother and their regular weekend fill-in guy, had become Allegany County's first recorded case of influenza, so he'd be unavailable to help this weekend. With Charlie, LuAnn and Les all in absentia, Brett would be hands-on for a couple of days at least.

Charlie and LuAnn Simmons were friends, employees and pseudo-parents, the kind of folks who made things better by just being themselves. Seeking solitude in his bungalow home behind the store, he'd watched the sales numbers rise over the summer. That was to be expected as travelers and tourists tooled down I-86.

But now?

He directed his gaze to the newly-created enterprise perched on the southwest corner. White twinkle lights blinked along the roofline of the former furniture factory's extended front facade, lighting antique-style cedar shingles with cozy brightness. Small trees winked in similar style, lining a parking lot that had been filled with cars until a short while ago. Customers had buzzed in and out all day, shopping nonstop. And some of those cars needed gas. Other shoppers needed food. Which meant the Crossroads did well.

The door opened. Brett turned.

Haley stood framed in the doorway, flanked by the two little boys, and if their expressions set the evening's tone, she had a long night in store. Tyler looked mutinous and the littler guy… Todd, he remembered… clutched the same scruffy, black stuffed cat that had been a mainstay at dinner yesterday.

"It's you."

She looked startled to see him, and maybe pleased? Brett hadn't been out of the game that long. Had he?

"It's me."

"Where are Charlie and LuAnn? And Steve? Or Ramir?" She answered her own question before Brett could jump in. "Jess must have had her baby! How wonderful. Oh, tell me, is it a boy or a girl?"

Her face transformed as she talked about the baby. While babies were all right, he preferred children of the walking/talking sort, the ones who could interact and occasionally amuse themselves. Like the two little guys before him. "It's a girl. Shelby Rose is her name…."

"Love it!" Haley beamed. Points of ivory made her eyes gleam, as if she'd stood in the "get sparkle here" line twice. The shine made the night less dark and damp, the persistent November rains less bothersome. She moved forward, smiling. "So they're help-ing with Michaela?"

"Yes. I guess she's excited to have a baby sister."

"Wonderful." Her smile said she approved, but then she dropped her attention to the boys at her side. "So, boys, what kind of sandwich would you like?"

"Nuggets."

"Me, too."

Haley's face reflected their predictability and her dismay. "The Crossroads doesn't have—"

Brett negated her argument with a hand up. "Watch me." He came around the counter, crossed the store, opened the wall freezer and withdrew a small, white box and hoisted it. "Nuggets."

Her look of relief made him feel ten feet tall and he tried not to notice that the forest-green peacoat layered over well-fitted blue jeans and heeled boots made her New York chic in small-town, USA. He decided there was something really good to be said about big-city looks. He directed his gaze down to the boys. "You guys want fries to go with that?"

"Yes!"

"Yes, please."

Brett bestowed a look of appreciation to Tyler. "You've got good manners, son. That's something to be proud of."

The boy's expression lightened. Brett felt a pull on his heart again. Whatever their story was, these boys had run the gamut, and at a young age. Not fair. Not fair at all, Brett decided as he dropped the nuggets and fries into the fryer baskets. He turned and faced Haley, trying not to think of how her tumble of long, blond curls set off the coat to perfection. He'd have to be asleep or dead not to have noticed them, and he was neither. "And how about you?"

She shook her head quickly. Too quick, Brett decided, then remembered her back-and-forth with LuAnn yesterday. She was short on funds.

He wasn't.

He leaned over the counter, braced his hands and held her gaze. "I know you've got leftovers at home. I'm going to bet that these two refused to eat them for Rory Madigan today."

Two guilty looks peeked up from below.

"And I'm going to surmise that you've worked all day and by the time you get the boys home, fed and into bed it will be nearly nine o'clock. So, consider this an order, not a question—what can I make you, Haley?"

The use of her name softened her jaw. She met his gaze, faltered, then caved. "May I have a chicken salad panini, please?"

He'd just cleaned the panini press, but yes, he'd make the sandwich for her and clean it again. Without grumbling. "Sure."

"With grapes?"

Did he hear her right? He started to turn when she added, "And chopped walnuts? Please?"

Fruit and nuts in chicken salad? On his panini grill?

"Charlie makes it for me all the time," she went

on, and Brett decided right then and there that Charlie might have some explaining to do with the cost of fruit and nuts crazy high this year. He reached for the loaf of Italian bread, but she caught his arm and sent sweet pings of attraction on an upward journey. "Oh, I'm sorry, Charlie always does my chicken salad on the rosemary focaccia bread, but you wouldn't have any way of knowing that, would you?"

He wouldn't because he'd spent the last two years keeping to himself, hiding in plain sight. His fault, he knew.

But he still meant to have a word or two with Charlie.

Haley darted quick glances to the pricing side of the lunch-board menu above him as he checked the nuggets and slid her sandwich into the press, prayed and locked the cover. The fryer bell signaled completion. He drained the fries and nuggets, piled them into two separate to-go containers, added dipping sauce, a pack of M&M's and a juice box.

Haley's eyes went round. She tripped over her words. "Um, we have drinks at home. The nuggets alone are fine, really. I, um…"

He ignored her protests, opened the panini press and smiled. No big mess, and the sandwich looked great. He flipped it onto the counter, cut it in half with a very manly carving knife, then slipped the grilled sandwich into a foam box for her, with a side of chips, her own miniature bag of M&M's and an empty cup for a drink.

"Oh, I—"

He handed the cup to Tyler. "Can you help Aunt Haley get a drink, please?" He turned his attention back to Haley. "I'm guessing she wants a Diet Coke."

She looked trapped and torn, but she followed Tyler to the soda bar, helped him hold the cup while she filled it, then let him assist again while they put a lid on it. She bent low and met Tyler's eye. "Can you carry this for me, please?"

He nodded, looking less combative and more self-confident. "Yes, ma'am."

Military manners, thought Brett. Polite. With good eye contact. Pretty impressive for a five-year-old.

Haley straightened, grabbed out a wallet and started fishing for a card. Brett raised his hands, holding her off. "No charge on that tonight, ma'am."

She stopped. Stared. Then shook her head and extended the card anyway.

Brett stepped back, steadfast. "No charge."

"But—"

"Just my way of welcoming the two newest citizens of Allegany County into the area."

"But what will Charlie say?"

Brett didn't choke. Obviously she thought Charlie and LuAnn owned the Crossroads. And her assumption was understandable because he'd kept to himself. When he wasn't helping his mother. Or working with the fire department.

The store was his post-army investment property. The mom-and-pop mini-store had transformed into a lucrative enterprise as Allegany County's economic woes diminished. Their recovery might be sluggish mid-winter, but the rest of the year? An upswing in business fed the cash register with a steady rise in income.

And after living on service pay minus careful investments for twenty-five years, Brett saw nothing wrong with a raise in salary.

He'd hired others to handle the store from the beginning, but being here today? Seeing the people, handling the orders, running the register for long hours? His hands-on involvement made him feel like he was part of something again. Between the Thanksgiving dinner yesterday and today's crazy-paced business, he'd felt fully involved in life for the first time in, well…too long. And he liked the feeling. "I'll fix it with Charlie."

She opened her mouth to argue and he fought the urge to silence her with two broad fingers against those sweet lips, just to see if she felt as good as she looked. Something told him she would. Common sense and decorum held him back. "It's fine. I promise."

Her heartfelt smile said she caved and the quick sheen of tears meant he'd touched a raw spot. "Go." He pointed toward the door. "Head home. Eat. Sleep. Tomorrow will be better." He dropped his gaze and winked at the two little camouflage-clad boys. "I promise."

"You have kids, Mr.…?"

"Brett," he told her. He came around the counter

and swung the door wide for them. "And no, I don't." The old stab of pain hit him mid-section, but without the usual gut-punch force. "Not married." He added that just in case she wondered. Maybe hoping she wondered. "But I *was* one, so I've got a pretty good take on things. Food. Play. More food. Bed."

"Thank you, Brett."

His heart stuttered as a seed of contentment nudged its way in. The way she said his name, kind of slow. Soft. The look of gratitude she sent him, that maybe said something more unless his skills had rusted from disuse.

"Come on, fellas. Let's get you home." She set the food on the passenger-side front seat, piled the boys into the car with greater ease than she'd displayed yesterday, and watched as Tyler tucked her cup into the cup holder. "Good job."

Her approval evoked the boy's smile, still tentative, but there.

Baby steps, Brett decided. He knew that regimen, all right.

He watched her pull away, then stared with surprise when she angled the car left, then right and pulled into the far right lot alongside the cooperative. A light blinked on in the back of the original furniture store. Then another.

She lived in the recently approved apartment behind the old furniture store. How had he missed that?

Then another thought occurred, bringing back her

conversation yesterday, her concern, the money issues, the time constraints.

He let his gaze wander Bennington Station, the new "Street of Shops"-type shopping experience enjoying a grand opening month to beat the band. Realization struck hard and deep.

She was Haley Jennings, Frederick Bennington's granddaughter, the mastermind behind the burgeoning enterprise spearheading new business opportunities and success in this corner of Allegany County.

And he was slated to do her fire safety inspection Monday morning.

The lights blinked, mocking him, as if daring him to find something wrong on Monday. Like she needed anything else on her plate right now.

But as interim inspector, the job was his while Bud Schmidt recovered from cancer surgery, and until then...

Haley Jennings would have to contend with him. He could only pray none of her merchants or subcontractors had messed up, but Brett knew the score. In the height of holiday shopping frenzy, everyone tried to use as much space as possible to promote themselves and their products. Improperly wired lighting displays, blocked exits, windows that wouldn't open with the rain or snow...

All things that could spell disaster. People hurt. Lives lost. Too often a little caution could have provided a totally different outcome.

He ground his jaw and wondered how he'd missed

her presence all these months, but the reality of that bit hard.

He'd been hiding, plain and simple. And the time for seclusion was over.

Chapter Three

Haley's cell phone buzzed as she clicked the bedroom door shut, wondering if little boys should bathe every night.

She hoped not.

She withdrew the phone, saw LuAnn's name and quickly answered. "LuAnn, hi. How's everything? Is Jess okay? And Shelby Rose? Is she doing fine?"

LuAnn's laugh held a hint of question. "Jess is fine, Michaela's excited, the baby's beautiful and has a healthy set of lungs just like her mother. How did you find out about her? I didn't want to call you at work because I knew how crazy today would be."

"Brett told me."

"*Brett* told you?" Surprise hiked the older woman's voice.

"The boys weren't exactly cooperative today, and by the time I got Rory home, they were starving. All those nice leftovers you provided for us yesterday? They won't touch them. And by eight o'clock at night,

I was too tired to fight it and not mean enough to starve 'em."

"So you stopped at the Crossroads for food."

"Brett made them nuggets and fries."

"He… What?" LuAnn's surprise pitched higher. "We don't have chicken nuggets at the Crossroads."

"I know." Haley breathed a sigh as she sank into the corner of her "new" resting place. She'd given the boys her big bed and taken the couch. She'd pretend the old cast-off sofa provided great support and she'd ignore the lumps, at least until life settled down after the holidays. Come January she should be able to breathe.

But she wasn't wishing the biggest shopping season of the year away. These eight weeks of sales provided enough profit for many to stay in business over the cold, dark days of a northern winter. She'd learned that in Lewisburg when she worked at the Street of Shops throughout her college years. She'd watched, listened and learned. When opportunity came her way in the shape of her grandfather's bequest of the somewhat-worn buildings, she was ready. She hoped.

"Well, I won't keep you, dear. I just wanted to say that Charlie and I will take the boys tomorrow. They can play here with Michaela and you're free to work as long as you need to."

Gratitude clogged Haley's throat. "LuAnn, that's a lovely gesture, but—"

"There'll be no buts," LuAnn cut in firmly. "We're two grown adults watching one little girl. Having the boys here will keep her busy. You're actually doing us a favor. Charlie is insisting that he's played the last game of Dora Memory in this lifetime, and because that's Michaela's current favorite, she wants to play it nonstop."

That information plugged another piece of the child-puzzle into Haley's thinking. "So that's normal for preschoolers?"

LuAnn laughed. "Absolutely. They grab on to a thought or a game and run with it repeatedly. Then they drop that and hang on to the next thing that takes their fancy. All quite normal, dear."

"And Todd's stuffed cat? Panther?" She said the little stuffed cat's name with a firm question mark attached. "It's not weird that he won't put it down? Ever? And gets really nervous when he does?"

"He's lost a great deal." LuAnn's voice went soft and reassuring. "Sometimes when we lose what we love, we cling tighter to what's left behind."

Words of wisdom. And that would explain why Todd mimicked Tyler repeatedly. There was safety in continuity, in same old, same old. Haley didn't know that from childhood experience. Her choppy upbringing held no horrid skeletons in the closet, but it didn't hold much substance either. And her mother would never understand why Haley drove straight to New Jersey when she'd heard of the boys' plight, grabbed the little fellows and brought them back to the Southern Tier of New York.

No. Her mother would have sent a generous check and moved on with her life, which made Haley more determined to distance herself from the money-is-everything mind-set her mother and stepfather embraced.

"Haley, are you still there?"

"Sorry, LuAnn. Just thinking. You know how dangerous that is for a blonde."

LuAnn laughed. "Not for you. I've never met a sweeter, funnier, smarter or more industrious young woman and I've been around a long time, Haley. You're one of a kind."

Oh, those words of affirmation. They sparked emotion in Haley. She blinked tears back and put the emotion on hold, a skill she'd learned long ago. She didn't know if indifference was as painful as physical trials and tribulations in childhood, but she understood the heartache of it firsthand.

An absentee father, an uncaring mother and a posh setting that pretended everything was all right. It had never been all right, but she'd moved up and out, determined to be her own person. This new enterprise achieved that, and made her proud. "LuAnn, you're sure it's not too much for you guys?"

"Because we're old?" LuAnn wondered out loud, laughing.

"No, because…" Haley tripped over her words, trying to backpeddle. She failed miserably. "I—"

"It will be fine, dear. Just fine. Charlie will swing by at eight o'clock. And if they're still in their jammies, just send clothes along. They can get dressed here."

Another reprieve. She had no idea that getting children dressed could be such an ordeal and wasn't sure if that was normal or not. Were they testing her?

Yes.

Were they winning?

She wrinkled her nose. So far, they were. And she couldn't deny she'd felt a certain sense of relief when she left the boys in Rory's capable hands that morning. Was that an understandable reaction or was she lacking the mother gene?

"Give it time, Haley." LuAnn's gentle wisdom uplifted her. "We live such fast-paced lives today that we forget to sit back. Be still. Breathe. Let things unfold."

"I feel pushed to hurry," Haley confessed, knowing LuAnn would somehow understand. "To achieve. To succeed."

"I think that's why the Psalms talk so much about patience." LuAnn's voice blanketed her. Warmed her from within. "To wait on the Lord. To stand strong and steadfast. But no one said it would be easy."

Haley got that, but right now, with two little souls suddenly dependent on her, a fledgling business to run and rising concern over the absence of that second bank draft in her business account, letting go and letting God proved to be a difficult concept. Maybe impossible. But once things settled down…

"Get some sleep," LuAnn advised. "Charlie will be there first thing."

"Thank you, LuAnn."

"You're welcome." LuAnn paused, but didn't hang up the phone. In a voice that sounded a touch off, she went back to the beginning of their conversation. "Did you really say that Brett made the boys chicken nuggets?"

"Yes. He totally saved the moment because I was facing mutiny."

"And Brett's our go-to person to defuse mutiny, that's for sure." LuAnn's tone mixed satisfaction with amusement. "Good night, dear."

"Good night."

Haley disconnected the call, grabbed the quilt she'd bought at Maude McGinnity's shop last summer, snugged her head into a not-so-comfortable throw pillow and promised herself a shopping trip soon. At least for a decent pillow to avoid the sore-neck headache she contended with today.

She'd get through tomorrow. Then Sunday. On Monday she'd hand over the reins of the co-op to one of the more experienced merchants and tackle the ever-growing to-do list, slightly annoyed that none of the tasks could be accomplished on her smartphone:

Sign Tyler up for school.

Find day care for Todd.

Talk to the bank officer and trace the delay on her loan.

Shop for food as funds allowed.

The fire inspection. She'd forgotten that the co-op was scheduled for another fire inspection Monday because the new wing was near completion. And with a busy weekend facing her, she didn't have extra time to make sure everything was perfectly spaced for the inspector.

But she'd have to because that was her job. She'd stay late Sunday and ask the merchants to check their own areas. Would they do it with her diligence?

Some would, some wouldn't. But with time growing short, she'd have to trust them to police their own areas for fire safety rules. The old showroom area had burned once, under suspicious circumstances, twenty years ago. She had no intention of letting her grandfather's legacy burn again.

Chapter Four

Brett's phone buzzed him awake shortly after 2:00 a.m. on Sunday morning, which made perfect sense because the bars closed right about then. He dragged himself awake, hating to take the call, knowing he had no choice. "Hey, Mom."

"Brett."

His throat tightened. His heart pinched. He knew that slur, that tone. "Where are you?"

"I'm home."

That might or might not be true. "Do you need a ride?"

"To where?"

He refused to sigh even though they'd traveled this ground often enough. "Home."

"But I am home."

The sound of raindrops and the movement of the occasional car said she wasn't. She needed a ride and was ashamed to ask. But she knew if she called, he'd figure it out. He always did. "I'll be right there. Which road are you on?"

She breathed deep, the sensitive mic telling him she was moving. Turning, maybe? Finding her bearings? "I'm near the library."

"In Wellsville?"

"Yes." The lisped word drained energy from his meager middle-of-the-night stash. "It's raining."

Pouring, actually. He grabbed a heavy jacket from a hook, his keys and a blanket to warm her. "I'm on my way. Go up the library stairs and wait. The rain can't soak you there."

"Okay."

She wouldn't do it. She'd be afraid someone would come along in the shadowed overhang. Find her. Make trouble. No, she'd feel more secure out by the street, with streetlights guiding her way, despite the teeming rain and lack of cover.

She hadn't called him in weeks. He'd hoped things were better. And he knew she'd gone to AA a couple of times, but he also knew overcoming addiction was hard work. Many a soldier under his command had fought addictive behaviors. Some succeeded. Some didn't.

But his mother's angst and depression made her a prime candidate, and she'd resumed old habits once his younger brother Ben had died in a military chopper training run over rugged California mountains.

Ben gone.

Joe gone.

And his mother had no one but him around to help pick up the pieces. She only called when desperate, but maybe this time he could make a difference. Maybe this time…

He headed through Jamison, the picturesque little town buttoned up for the night. The Highway Department had strung lights and affixed wreaths on old-style lampposts. The whimsical effect proffered charm and invitation, and Jamison specialized in charismatic appeal. But tonight the prettiness of the Christmas season mocked him. He'd let down his son. His brother. And his mother wanted little to do with him most days.

But that hadn't changed much in four decades, so he wasn't exactly looking for a miracle. More like peace of mind. Atonement.

He pulled up to the library fifteen minutes later and found no sign of Joanna Stanton anywhere.

He parked the SUV, climbed out and took the library steps at a quick clip, but no one waited under the overhang.

"Mom?"

He kept his voice soft and low. The neighbors living along North Main Street wouldn't appreciate being awakened at three in the morning. "Mom?"

Nothing.

He took out his phone and punched in her number on his speed dial.

"Hellooo?"

"Mom, where are you?"

"Who is this?"

Brett hauled in a breath, looked around and still

couldn't find her. "It's Brett. You called me for a ride. I'm here at the library in Wellsville. Where are you?"

She hiccupped. "In Wellsville? At this hour? Why?"

"Because you called me."

"Did I?" A long pause stretched thin before she spoke again. "Oh, I got a ride, but thank you very much for calling."

Click.

She got a ride?

From whom?

And where was she now?

He climbed back into the SUV and headed toward her apartment complex on the north side of town, then idled the engine outside, debating a course of action.

No lights. No movement.

He rang the bell, but wasn't sure how far to go. Was she in there, passed out? Had some good Samaritan taken her home? Or had she decided to spend the remainder of an awful night with someone from the bar?

He had no way of knowing, and not enough information to call 9-1-1. His mother was a grown woman with choices. He wished she'd make better ones, but that hadn't happened while he was growing up. And her fifteen-year stint of sobriety had ended with Ben's death.

He got back into the SUV, drove home, gave up on the idea of sleep, stared at his bookshelves and moved right past the row of books on how to be a better person, settled on a new action thriller and pretended his mother was safe and sound in her apartment, cozy and warm.

It was a form of make-believe he employed in childhood. It didn't work any better now that he was a man.

No way would she make it to the church on time. Or even close, Haley determined as the boys took forever to get ready.

"Do we haaaaave to go?" Tyler whined. "I'd rather stay home and play with toys."

"Me, too." Todd plunked himself down and sent her a most serious look. "I don't want to go to stupid old church. Ever."

"Church isn't stupid," Haley corrected Todd as she grabbed his coat from the back of a chair and tossed Tyler's across the small sofa. "It's nice."

Tyler snorted.

Todd followed suit.

Neither made a move to put their coats on.

Haley decided reasoning might help. "And you've never been to this church—"

"We've never been to any church," Tyler interrupted. He folded his arms and braced his legs, a miniature man-in-the-making and too stubborn for his own good. "And if my mom and dad wanted me to go to church, they'd have taken me."

Not to be outdone, Todd mimicked the action and the out-thrust lower jaw. "Me, too."

Nothing in Psych 101 prepared Haley to argue with

Tyler. So she wouldn't. "Mom and Dad were busy. I'm not. Therefore we're going to church."

"But!"

"But!"

"No buts. My house. My rules. And Sunday morning is time for God. For worship. For music."

"Could just get a stupid radio," Tyler muttered, but he grabbed his jacket, slung it over his head and opened the door.

"I hate this jacket," Todd whined as Haley bent to help him connect the zipper. "It's dumb. And Panther doesn't like it either."

"Inanimate objects can't be dumb, but it is a pain-in-the-neck zipper. And I think you've almost outgrown it, kid. And Panther's a pretty smart cat." She directed her gaze down to the worn stuffed animal. "He wants you warm."

"Really?" Todd's face lit up. "Well, that's nice." He clutched the black cat tighter. "I can get a new coat maybe?"

"As soon as I find time to shop," Haley promised. She'd checked her bank account that morning. No transfer of funds as yet, and that meant she'd still have to invent time in her Monday schedule to find out why the second draft of the bank loan hadn't been initiated. Concern tweaked her. What if the bank backed out? What if they wanted to renegotiate terms? Would her lawyer charge her more? Would the bank do that? Could they do that?

She wasn't sure, which meant she'd be working

under a cloud the rest of the day, wondering. Waiting. Hoping the draft would be released in time to pay her subcontractors by midweek. Contracted workers didn't take kindly to being stiffed anytime of year, but at Christmas? While finishing up the final phase of a large contract?

Praying nothing was amiss, she got the boys into the car, drove the three-quarters of a mile into Jamison, found a parking spot and realized she'd be almost twenty minutes late for the first service at Good Shepherd, but ten minutes early for the White Church at the Bend.

The ticking clock spelled victory for the White Church.

She grasped a little-boy hand in each of hers and climbed the steps, glad the steady rain had given it a rest, at least for now.

"Haley."

Matt Cavanaugh's voice welcomed her as she and the boys entered the newly refinished church. Matt had been her initial contractor for Bennington Station, and he was paid in full, so she didn't have to feel embarrassed to see him, an emotion she loathed. "Matt. Callie. How nice to see you guys."

Matt Cavanaugh gave her a half hug, then squatted low to meet the boys. "You must be Tyler."

Tyler nodded, shy but not too taken aback.

"And you're Todd."

"I'm free." Todd wriggled three chubby fingers into the air like a beacon, his other hand clutching Panther.

"Three?" Matt's face displayed wide-eyed appreciation for that bit of information. "Great age, buddy. This is my wife, Callie." He stepped back as his wife smiled down at the boys. "And our son, Jake. And our daughter, Morgan."

"A baby," Tyler noted, unimpressed.

"We like babies," Todd insisted.

"*You* do," Tyler argued. His arms clenched his middle again. "I don't. They smell."

"Um, well, that's enough now, boys." Haley made a face at Callie and Callie laughed, shrugging it off. The newborn baby girl in Matt's arms slept on, unfazed by the boy's gruff appraisal.

"They're just at that age where if it pops in their head, it comes out their mouth," Callie explained. "No filter."

"You've got that right." Haley sent a wistful glance Jake's way. "So it gets better, right? Because Jake is always a sweetheart and he's what? Nine? Ten?"

"Nine. And yes, it gets better." Callie Cavanaugh reached out and gave Haley a hug. "Promise. And it's nice to see you over here. Si will have something to hold over Reverend Hannity's head when the reverend realizes you came here."

"Timing." Haley aimed her gaze to the boys and her watch. "We'll start earlier next week, but I like coming here sometimes. Listening to Simon. He's a character."

Matt laughed. "And then some. And you like the upgrades to the church?"

Haley swept the refreshed church a look and offered

Matt a shoulder chuck. "You're fishing for compliments when you know you did great. Yes, between the new roof and the plaster and paint, it's a huge difference. But mostly I love what you did with the pews. Cleaning them. Lightening them." She stroked a hand across the broad-backed oak seating. "It's beautiful."

Matt smiled at her, but then his attention shifted up. Way up. "Brett, hey. How's everything? Good to see you."

Haley's heart fluttered, hoping there was only one Brett in town. Heat suffused her cheeks in a childish reaction that felt silly and good all at once.

She turned. Looked up. Her good intentions flew out the window, a neat trick because the cold rain meant no windows were open.

He looked marvelous. Tall. Broad. Freshly shaved. He wore a charcoal, tan and brown tweed jacket over a blended-brown turtleneck that matched his hazel eyes. He was, by definition, gorgeous, and she'd love to pretend he wasn't, but acting had never been her forte. He looked down, caught her eye and smiled.

Just smiled.

But that smile held her gaze and put a choke hold on her heart despite the fact that they'd met only days before. She couldn't break the look if she tried, and she really didn't want to try, but people began seating themselves around them, getting ready for worship.

Which was exactly why she'd come, right? To give the boys a taste of faith. Of family. Of community.

With Brett Stanton so close, the only thing she could

wrap her mind around was wondering how a man this big, strong and rugged hadn't been married off yet. These days, that should raise flags of concern, but not with him. And that made her wonder why.

A soft guitar strum reminded her to find a seat.

Brett stepped back, motioned a hand left and let her and the boys file into the filling pew. There wasn't enough room for all four of them, and she realized too late he'd given up his seat for her and the boys, but when she turned to thank him, he was gone, into the back, seated quietly in the last row.

"And the first shall be last."

He didn't look her way or blanket her with another smile, but it felt good to have him there. To know he sat nearby.

She was willing to rise to a challenge, Brett decided. He'd suspected as much, but seeing her this morning, with the boys' stubborn little chins set in determined objection, he knew she had what it takes to make this parenting gig work. But a little help from some friends couldn't hurt.

You're not her friend, his conscience scolded.

But I will be, Brett decided. Pastor Simon MacDaniel strolled into the polished and reconditioned sanctuary, and Brett realized two things. One, that Simon's gentle charismatic nature was drawing more people every week, and two...

That it would take more than Simon's charm to make him forget that Haley Jennings and two needy little boys sat a mere thirty feet away. If her tumble of golden hair wasn't enough of a distraction, Todd's little smile, turned just toward him, clinched the deal.

He'd make it easy and pray for her and the boys today. Concentrate his efforts. And with the sweet smile she'd raised in his direction, it wouldn't be a hard task at all.

Simon grinned at Haley after the service and waved a hand toward Good Shepherd Church across the Park Round. "Wait 'til Reverend Hannity hears about this."

"Trouble maker." She grinned up at him, then slanted her gaze to the boys. "Pastor Si, these are my nephews, Tyler—" she indicated the older boy by raising their linked hands "—and Todd. They've come to live with me."

Simon squatted low to speak to them. "Nice to meet you both." He put out a hand to each boy in turn, shook theirs, then angled his gaze up toward Haley. "We're having coffee and doughnuts in the common room downstairs."

Haley winced, hesitating. The co-op was slated to open at noon and she needed to be there. As yet, she had no one to watch the boys. Jess was bringing the baby home today and Charlie and LuAnn needed to be on hand to help their daughter and son-in-law. Her cousin Alyssa Michaels was working at The Edge, their family restaurant, and Alyssa's husband, Trent, was coaching football for their teenaged son. That meant the boys would be going with her to Bennington Station, a solution that ranked dead last on her list of preferences.

"I like doughnuts." Tyler sent a wistful look upward.

"I love them this much." Todd opened his arms wide, the black kitty clutched tightly in his outstretched fingers. "Panther does, too."

"Haley."

That voice. The tone. The deep rumble that stirred things she didn't know existed before Thanksgiving Day. She turned, swallowing hard, pretty sure she'd trip over anything she might try to say. "Yes?"

He reached down and scooped Todd up. The boy giggled, delighted with his new, high vantage point. Brett settled a big, broad hand on Tyler's head in a gentle move of inclusion. "Come have coffee and doughnuts, leave the boys with me for the afternoon so you can work and then you won't be either kicking yourself or second-guessing yourself for the next six hours."

"Could we?" Tyler looked excited by the prospect of hanging out with Brett, but Haley barely knew this man.

"I would wuv that!" Todd beamed a smile at Brett and then bumped his little head into Brett's forehead in a mini-man gesture of salute. "Can we play at your house?"

"I have trains," Brett told him.

"Trains?" Tyler frowned, wondering.

"Trains?" Todd repeated, mimicking his brother.

"Brett has an amazing collection of model trains,"

Si told them. "And he's got a few that are kid-friendly size, if I remember correctly."

"I do." Brett switched his look from Simon to Haley. "If that's okay with you, Haley. The boys can hang out with me and the dog...."

"You have a dog?"

"A real dog?"

"Very real." Brett nodded, serious, but his eyes twinkled down at Haley. "We'll be right across the street, so you can run over if you get worried or have time on your hands."

"You live near Charlie and LuAnn's store?"

Simon coughed.

Brett sent him a look, then hiked up the shoulder that wasn't holding Todd. "It's actually my store, and yes, I live in the house behind it."

"Really?" If that was true, why hadn't she run into him before Thanksgiving?

He rolled his eyes toward Simon. "I do believe that's what I said. Come on." He headed toward the stairs. "Let's grab some coffee, feed these guys one of Seb Walker's doughnuts and get you to work. Then the boys and I can have some fun."

She shouldn't, should she? Was this the height of irresponsibility to leave two little boys with a virtual stranger?

Trust your heart. Go with your instincts.

She was good at that professionally, but this wasn't a business proposition. These were her brother's boys, now her own little ones. One look at the integrity in

Brett's strong, rugged face put her fears to rest. Something in his bearing said she could trust him with anything. Anytime. And that was the nicest feeling she'd had in years.

He read her hesitation and waited her out, no tempting. No cajoling. She appreciated the honor that took, so she nodded, grabbed Tyler's hand and moved downstairs. "That would be lovely, Brett."

She glanced over her shoulder and read the smile he sent for her. Just for her. And suddenly her crazy day melted away into something simpler. Sweeter. She could go to work and not worry about the boys.

Her bank loan?

There was nothing to do about that until tomorrow, so today she'd work with the peace of mind that the boys were well-cared for. And the fact that she'd get to see Brett again later, when she picked up the boys?

Only made the day that much brighter.

Chapter Five

Football, napping boys and trains.

Only one thing could make this afternoon better, Brett decided as the boys snuggled along his dog Derringer's tawny-red wide flank, and she knocked on the door about five-fifteen, the cold rain beating a relentless rhythm against the flagstone walk. Brett hurried to the door, knowing Haley was getting soaked on the open stoop. "Get in here. It's pouring."

"Tell me something I don't know." She shook damp tendrils out of her face as she pushed back the Christmas-toned knit scarf. "Who'd have thought you could get this wet running from the car?"

"Here." He lobbed a towel her way, then hooked a thumb left. "Come this way, but be quiet."

"Because?"

He didn't answer. If he told her why he wanted her to follow him, she'd offer some form of protest. Better to have the upper hand, he decided. Ward off the argument. She came up behind him and he shifted to the right to allow her a better vantage point.

Her face softened. Her mouth formed a perfect O, the soft lips looking sweet and inviting, which almost made Brett feel guilty about setting a perfect scene, but he'd been straight-up army for a long time. Tactical precision was a specialty.

"How sweet."

"Yup."

"And the dog…"

"Derringer."

"Oh, Brett." She hugged his arm and this time he didn't resist the temptation to slip an arm around her shoulders. Gaze down into her face. Wonder what it would be like to touch his mouth to hers. "They look so peaceful."

"A shame to wake them."

She smiled up at him, and the glance to his mouth told him she was pondering a similar course of action. It would take seconds to find out. A space of mere inches to test the waters…

"I wuv this dog, Brett."

Todd's voice interrupted the moment but didn't detract from the sweetness. He sat up, fisted his sleepy eyes and then rubbed a generous spot on the coonhound's side. "He's the best dog ever."

"He is." Brett offered Haley's shoulder a little squeeze that said "next time." He moved across the room and squatted. He stroked the dog's neck, turned and smiled up at Haley. "He used to be Charlie and

LuAnn's. They moved to a place with less upkeep but the old boy was too big for the community rules. I took him in and that way LuAnn's with him most of the time."

"He's beautiful." She crossed the room and bent low to pet the dog. She smelled of cinnamon and evergreen, a delicious combination, the scents drawing him in as if her effusive personality and good looks weren't enough.

She's beginning her life. You've seen half of yours and messed up a good share of that. Leave her be.

He should. He knew that. But when she slanted a look his way, a look that brought her cheek dangerously close, he had to reach out. Brush tendrils of hair back behind her ear. See if the soft skin of her cheek was velvet or satin.

A little of both, he decided, smiling at her.

The dog rolled, pawed the air, groaned and woke Tyler with his movement.

"Oh, that's funny!" Todd fell down laughing at the sight of the big dog groaning in his sleep as Tyler slid off to the left.

"Ouch."

Brett reached out an arm to Tyler, scooped him up and rubbed the spot that landed on the rug. "Rough way to wake up, huh? Did you have a good nap?"

"I don't take naps."

"As a rule." Brett carried him into the kitchen and set him on the counter. He examined Tyler's head and stepped back. "I don't think it needs ice, do you?"

The boy contemplated the question, then shrugged. "Naw. And Derringer didn't mean to do it."

"No."

"He was just rolling over, right?"

"Right."

"And he likes kids."

"Hasn't eaten one yet." Brett offered that response with an easy grin.

Tyler replied in kind. "But the day ain't over."

"You're learning, kid. Hey, how about you and Todd set the table so we can have some supper?"

"Oh, Brett, thank you, but—" Haley offered the protest, but he'd already figured out she didn't accept help easily and that probably had a story behind it. Well, who didn't have a story? Considering her current circumstances, he was determined to help because it was advantageous to her and…

If he was being honest with himself…

Just being with her felt good to him. End of discussion.

"No buts." He flashed an over-the-shoulder smile her way, but didn't pretend he'd take no for an answer. The boys had to eat and so did she, even if resistance was her first line of defense. For an established soldier like him, it wasn't much of a battle. "If your entrepreneurial nature must be kept busy 24/7, then help the boys set the table. Plates are there." He shifted his chin up and to the left. "Silverware in the drawer next to the sink. And cups are above the plates."

"But—"

He sent her a look that quashed her protest much like it had with troops at home and abroad, and decided that look might come in handy. Or maybe he hoped it would come in handy. Either way, her response was to help the boys while he poured pasta into a pot of salted, boiling water.

"You cooked for us?"

"Way easier than cooking for a legion of troops." He handed her a loaf of crusty bread from the deli area of the store. "And I did that often enough as I worked my way up the ranks."

"You served."

"Twenty-five years."

"Army?"

"Yup."

"Wow." She turned and stared straight at him, and a part of him hoped the surprise wasn't because that made him seem really old. Because no way did he want her thinking he was too old. Or off his game. Which was ridiculous because he was both, but right now, here, with her, he didn't want to be.

She stepped his way and lay a cool, slim hand against his cheek. "Thank you for doing that."

"I was young when I signed up."

His words made her flash him a knowing smile. Kind of flirty. And fun.

"Real young." He added the qualifier in a deep, rugged tone, driving his point home. It worked. She grinned.

"Barely out of diapers, no doubt."

"Well." He hedged that one slightly. "Barely old enough to drive, at any rate."

"So I shouldn't think of you as old," she mused aloud as she set out silverware. "Just seasoned."

"Exactly."

"Or aged, like vintage wine."

"I like seasoned better."

"So do I." She turned and met his look full on and he realized right there and then that his age meant little to her and that felt good. "My mother used to say I was like a little old woman, old before my time."

"Was that a compliment?"

The look she sent him said more than the word. "No."

"Ah." He brought over a big bowl of red sauce and meatballs, but decided they'd share stories another time. Maybe. "Luckily I like mature women."

She laughed out loud.

He liked that she let herself react to a given situation. She didn't mince words or pretend, she reacted, and while these days that wasn't considered socially advantageous, he found her spontaneity contagious. And inspiring.

"I'm so hungry." Tyler sucked in a deep breath of sauce-scented air. "Brett, I think you're a really good cooker."

"Well, thank you." He pulled out a chair for Haley and that simple, gentlemanly gesture delighted her. He read it in her face, her smile, her eyes. Her look of pleasure made him feel taller. Broader. Nicer.

And somewhat adolescent.

He helped Todd settle himself into the chair, then drained the pasta into a strainer too small to hold the whole pot.

"Not exactly accustomed to cooking for a crew, huh?"

He shot Haley a grin. "As you'll note by the mismatched plates and silverware, LuAnn outfitted me with whatever leftover spoils she had in her kitchen. When you're on your own, it doesn't make sense to spend money on things. If I'm eating alone, I can pick any plate I want and it doesn't need to match anything else."

"Matching is overrated," she assured him as she held up her fork and her knife.

"Good girl."

She preened his way and he had to stop himself from reaching out. Touching her. Damp tendrils of hair were drying in the heat of the small kitchen, leaving curls in their wake, and the sight of those curls made him wonder what it might be like to have a little girl some day, a tiny girl with a head full of blond ringlets. And because he'd never in his life entertained thoughts like this, the fear might have overwhelmed the enticement of home, family and forever if she hadn't held his gaze with the warm, open smile that was simply Haley Jennings. But she did and he felt like a superhero as a result.

"I love sketti." Todd started to dive into the bowl of pasta before him, but Haley held up a hand of caution.

"Grace first."

"Aww…"

"Do we—"

Brett solved the objections by taking Tyler's hand on one side and folding Haley's into his on the other. Soft, slim and tapered, her fingers fit as if meant to be tucked inside his bigger, broader hands. Once they'd completed the circle he offered a quick grace, pretty sure starving boys wouldn't sit still for a longer version.

"Nice timing." Haley confirmed his decision with a quick glance toward Todd. He was busily scooping bow-shaped pasta as fast as his spoon allowed.

"Makes me glad I didn't pick real spaghetti." Brett indicated Todd with his look. "Although that would be a camera-ready event, I expect."

"I'm sure you're right." She took another forkful of pasta and meatballs and sighed. "Brett, thank you for this. And for last night. And for just being you."

Brett shrugged off her thanks. "None needed. Had to welcome our two little guys, didn't I?"

Her quick smile lit up a dusk-filled corner of his heart. Maybe his soul. Although he wasn't sure he had one anymore. Not that he wasn't a praying man. No one faced the enemy as often or as steadfastly as the United States Army, and that made a man take mortality seriously. And God more so.

But while God had kept him safe from harm, his love of the military inspired two people to enlist. Both had lost their lives. Not God's fault. Not the army's fault either. But he should have known better. As the older brother of one and the father of the other, he bore the weight of both.

"You look tired." Haley's blue eyes softened, then crinkled in concern. "Are you okay?"

"Missed some sleep last night. Nothing strange about that."

"There was no fire call last night."

He sent her a look that wondered where she got the information and drawled out his response. "True."

"I know that because Lisa Fitzgerald has a Christmas greens store in the co-op and I asked her about you. Because that's what girls do," she explained, smiling. "Who needs Google when we've got small-town backyard gossip?" She ignored his little groan, ate another spoonful, then went on. "The Ladies' Auxiliary teams up with Lisa for all kinds of things. Weed stealing. Pink parties. Flower sales."

"So you were on an info mission?" He tipped a grin her way. "Find out anything that put you off? Although Lisa actually likes me because I let her use the corner spot to sell flowers in season and that way she has both sides of town covered for the interstate access. And that weed-stealing crew is nothing to mess with. You can't find a better bunch of people who get the job done, no muss, no fuss. But I still find it noteworthy that I became the topic of conversation, Haley."

She smiled as if talking about him meant something. But in a small town, everyone talked about everyone. Except him. Which made this concept intriguing because women could ferret out covert information faster than Fort Bragg's finest.

"We were just talking and your name came up."

"Because?"

Her deepening flush inspired his grin and Brett had a hard time remembering the last time he grinned at a pretty girl on purpose. He'd kept himself off the beaten path since retiring from the army, and in spite of no small number of casseroles, brownies and invites finding their way to his door, he'd managed to stay beneath the radar.

Currently being in the radar's scope didn't seem all that bad. But the very thought of her being interested in a crusty curmudgeon like him bordered on ludicrous. Crazy, even. At least highly unlikely.

One glance into her sparkling eyes said it might not be all that implausible.

That's lack of sleep talking. You're old, she's young. You're hardened, she's ingenuous. You could use a shower and a shave and she's, well...beautiful. Sweet. Clean. Fresh.

All reasons enough to steer clear of Haley Jennings and her two protégés. He had plenty on his plate right now. More than enough. His business. His current task as fire code inspector. His work as a volunteer fireman. His ongoing problems with his mother.

That reality darkened his mind and the thought must have shaded his face because Haley leaned over, concerned. "I am grateful, Brett. For your kindness and your time. Your generosity last night, even though I thought you were pretty handy at giving away Charlie's stuff."

He grinned and shrugged. "No big deal, Haley."

"It was to me." She lay her hand over his and held his gaze. "It was the light I needed in a convoluted day."

Her words touched him. Coupled with the soft grasp of her fingers against the back of his hand, warm emotion multiplied by a factor of at least eight. He stowed the emotion and tipped his gaze.

He longed to be a light in someone's day, but hadn't realized it until Haley slipped into his life on a cloudy, windswept Thanksgiving. He shrugged one shoulder, refusing to make a big deal out of common courtesy. "Then I'm glad."

He waved off her help after dinner with a look in the boys' direction. "You'll have enough to do once you get them home."

"We don't have a home."

Tyler's words hit their mark. Haley's face paled. Todd's lip trembled. And Brett realized how vulnerable these two little fellows were right now, so he bent low and drew Tyler up into his arms. "It feels like that now, Ty. But give it time, okay?" He headbutted the little boy gently. "We'll give it time together and we'll play and pray and eat and have fun and after a while it will feel more like home. I promise."

The boy's face said he longed to believe but didn't dare, and Brett understood his reluctance. When dreams get knocked down regularly, it's hard to grasp hold. But Tyler was young. They'd convince him.

Haley reached out a gentle, practical hand. "You're right, Brett." She palmed Tyler's cheek and smiled. "'To everything there is a season and a time to every purpose under the heaven.'" She stretched up and whisked butterfly kisses along Tyler's cheek. "Time helps, Ty."

The little guy didn't look convinced, but he didn't look combative either and that was a step up. Brett walked Tyler out to Haley's car. The rain had let up slightly, but the steady drizzle was still enough to soak his sweatshirt while Ty and Todd got buckled.

"Thank you, Brett."

The smile she sent him over the hood of the car said more, but Tyler's words made him realize they needed to ease their way because these boys had already lost so much. He waved and backstepped his way toward the house behind him. "Get in. Get home. Dry off. Again."

She ducked into the car, put it in reverse and backed out of his drive, but he took sweet comfort in the fact that she traveled only four hundred feet down the road before turning into the back entrance of Bennington Station. Knowing she was this close? That he could be of help at a moment's notice?

He liked that proximity. A lot.

Chapter Six

"You're kidding, right?" Haley stared at the woman in the main office of the Jamison Central Public School and prayed she'd heard wrong. "I can't just sign Tyler up for school?"

Tyler's expression said he wasn't surprised. For a little kid, he'd been refused and rebuffed for months. Why should today be any different? And why didn't she think of finding someone to watch them this morning? She'd figured she would march in here, fill out papers, hand Ty his lunch and be on her way.

Wrong. Wrong. Wrong.

"Vaccination papers." She repeated the secretary's words and pursed her lips, confused. "Do I get them from a doctor here? Would he have already had them? Who would know?"

The woman shrugged. Her face showed compassion, but the law allowed no leeway. "Check with whoever had him previously. His former caretaker."

"Aunt Dell," offered Tyler. Discouragement colored his tone.

Haley sent Ty a reassuring smile. "Thanks, Ty. I'll give her a call."

"Won't do any good." He slouched down in his seat with an air of dejection. "She don't answer her phone. Says she don't like to talk to people 'cept in person."

"Doesn't answer her phone," Haley gently corrected, then palmed a hand over his head. "We'll figure this out, Ty. I promise. I just didn't know it was required," she explained to the woman at the desk. "The boys just came to live with me on Thanksgiving, so it was impossible to get anything done on a holiday weekend."

"I understand." The woman held out a short list to Haley. "Here are the names of a few local family doctors and two pediatricians in Wellsville. They'll be able to walk you through the process, but the guardianship papers need to be approved by a New York court."

"And I have no idea how to do that." Haley glanced at the clock, wishing the hours back. She'd been trying to settle the boys in since eight-thirty and the clock was stretching toward ten. She still had to visit the day care center Alyssa told her about for Todd and get to her noon appointment at the bank in Wellsville. Her fire inspection was slated for one-thirty and even though she'd warned the vendors, she knew everyone was in recovery mode after the busiest shopping weekend of the year. Fatigue might lead to carelessness, something she couldn't afford to have a fire inspector find. But she was here and the co-op would have to wait.

Haley didn't do waiting well.

Impatience snaked up her spine. Acceptance was about last on her list of attributes when it came to business. This was where a gung-ho attitude could get her into trouble, but right now she was caught trying to iron out legalities for the two boys and that was more important than anything else. She knew that.

But the clock ticked on.

"I'll figure this out, contact one or more of these—" she waved the papers toward the woman, grabbed Todd's hand and nodded to Tyler to get up "—and get back to you. Hopefully soon so we can get this fellow started."

"We'd like that." The woman settled a gentle smile on the boys, a warm look of acceptance and grace. "And boys, I love your camouflage jackets. My boys loved to wear camo when they were little and my grandsons love it, too. You remind me of them."

"Did their dad die, too? And their mom?" Todd voiced the question with all the innocence a three-year-old could muster.

Haley's throat seized. Her chin went lax. Two little boys should never have to go through this. Any of this. The loss of parents, the shuffling around, the lack of structure, silly legalities blocking their way from a nice, normal existence.

The other woman took a deep breath. A sheen of tears brightened her eyes, but she shook her head.

"No, but every night I thank God for people just like your daddy and mommy. People who try so hard to be good and fight for our freedom." She tapped the form listing Anthony's name and rank. "Your daddy was a hero for being a soldier, and your mommy was a hero for being strong while he was gone."

That made sense to Todd.

Tyler didn't look as certain. "But Mommy cried a lot when Daddy died. Aunt Dell kept telling her to find a job and things would get better, but Mommy said it wasn't that easy. They fought a lot."

Haley's heart broke.

How she wished Angi had called her. Moved up here. Spent time in a community that truly looked after its own. Reality told her that Angi barely knew her, but Angi's family had never been strong. Or supportive. Or even all that nice.

Thank You, God, for sending the boys here. For Great-Aunt Theresa finding Anthony's will. For giving us this chance to make a difference in Todd and Tyler's life. And please, please, please: Help me figure out all this legal stuff because I've got no clue what I'm doing.

She led the boys back to the car, headed for the clean, bright and fenced day care facility and was considerably less surprised to find out she needed Todd's medical records, too.

Strike two.

Strike three came when the bank officer explained that the second draft of the loan would be transferred into her business account as soon as she got a clean fire inspection that afternoon.

Which was in approximately thirty minutes, and she was twenty minutes away with two hungry boys, no babysitter and no prep time for the fire inspection.

Haley was never unprepared. Ever. She thought nothing of losing sleep, food or free time to get the job done and get it done right, so being caught unprepared for this fire inspection spiked her ire.

And when Brett Stanton walked in the door with an official-looking notepad at one twenty-seven, she wanted to curl up and hide.

Brett's opinion mattered to her. A lot. Something about him, his solidity, his strength, the sheer force of the man drew her. Balanced her.

And here he was as the fire inspector, with a job to do. Haley considered herself an accurate judge of character. Getting to know Brett these past few days told her one thing: He did his job well. And that might be her undoing.

His presence unnerved her.

This time it wasn't because of mutual flirtation. Today he blamed the notepad. And his official capacity as her fire inspector.

She wasn't ready. And he wished he could walk out the door, give her a reprieve of time, but he couldn't. And if she wasn't prepared for a scheduled inspection, what would happen when he or Bud Schmidt popped in for an impromptu check?

He read her expression, appraised the situation and then did what he was paid to do with more reluctance than he ever thought possible.

"Haley."

"Brett." She stared up at him, squared her shoulders and blew out a breath.

"Rough morning?"

"You could say that." She pointed to where the boys sat with a vendor in the small retro-styled dining café to their right.

"No school for Tyler?" Brett turned her way, concerned.

"Not without court-approved guardianship papers and vaccination records."

"None of which you have."

"Exactly." She breathed deep, made a face and shrugged. "And Todd can't start in the day care without vaccination records either. And Tyler assures me that Aunt Dell won't answer her phone to talk to me, that she won't talk to anyone on the phone and I have no idea how to get hold of any records of any kind. Angi's family isn't exactly forthcoming."

"I see."

Her gaze went stormy. Her eyes glimmered, but she held tight, shoulders back. "And my bank draft is being held up until we get our clean fire inspection and I wasn't here to see to the details this morning, so I'm going to bet that we'll have things to fix and you'll have to come back to reinspect."

"It happens all the time." He offered the words as

assurance, but from the look on her face he knew she was reaching a breaking point. She'd had day after day of dealing with her new role as caregiver, her new business, the lack of sleep and problems inherent to both and unless he missed his guess, her money had run dry. But he had a job to do, and until that was done, he had no way to offer help. So… "Let's get this done. See where we stand. And then we'll go from there."

"Fine."

Her stubborn look almost made him smile, but he had a narrow line to walk today. That of a new friend willing to help and that of a commissioned inspector with a job to do. A job he didn't take lightly as a volunteer fireman. Fire safety was of huge importance and despite her tumultuous weekend, this was an essential detail of business, especially in the north where winter fires claimed lives annually. Brett hated that lack of caution and common sense could cost lives. "Will you accompany me?"

"Of course."

The opening area looked fine. He went through with nothing to note, but when he got into the main vendor area of the old furniture factory, he knew he was in trouble. Over-the-top lighting displays drew his first tag. Aisles made thin by excess product. Flammable materials set near candles with used wicks. His list grew and by the time they got into the antiques floor upstairs, he figured she'd burst into tears.

But when he looked her way, she wasn't despondent. Mad, yes. Depressed? No.

And once again he realized that Haley went above and beyond the usual. His heart opened a little more, while he finished the list of citations.

"How long do we have to clean up our act?" She faced him straightforward, her face ready to do battle. But not with him, and that relieved him tenfold.

"Two weeks."

She shook her head. "I can't wait that long, but I heartily apologize for putting you through a senseless inspection. Can you come back Wednesday?"

Her determination made him proud, but there was no way he could make it back on Wednesday with two full inspections on new housing at the opposite end of the county. But those were the last two on his docket between now and New Year's and Bud Schmidt might be back on duty the first of the year, depending on his prognosis and healing. "No, but Thursday?"

"Thursday will be fine." She led the way to the broad, old stairs leading down to the first floor. At the bottom, she turned again, extending her hand. "Thank you, Brett."

"Haley, I—"

He wasn't sure what he wanted to say, but never got the chance because the boys caught sight of him and raced their way.

"Brett!"

"Hey, Brett!"

He caught Todd up, rubbed foreheads with the little

fellow and then noogied Tyler's head. "What have you guys got going this afternoon?"

"Nothing."

"Nothin'."

"How about you come with me so Aunt Haley can get things done."

She shook her head, but the boys' clamor made it academic. "Brett, really, I—"

"Do you have another option?"

"No." She scowled and tapped her foot. "And I've got plenty to do here." She waved the citation sheet with more intensity than necessary, making him choke back a smile again.

"You stay here and get things worked out," he told her. "I'll take the boys and do a little shopping. Keep them busy. We'll get them ready for an upstate winter."

Her face showed misgiving, a look he read easily, but the boys' fleece hoodies wouldn't cut it now. The forecast called for snow, snow and more snow by the following week. The kids needed to be ready. "You can pay me back once you've got solid ground beneath your feet again. But for now they need stuff and we can't afford to wait until you can replenish your accounts with the bank draft if it's going to take days to be awarded."

"Can I get my new coat?" wondered Todd out loud.

Brett met Todd's eye. "Yes."

"And me, too?"

"Yes. We'll get that all ironed out because when you do start school, you need to be prepared."

"With, like…new clothes? Really?" Tyler offered Brett a look that drew open his soldier's heart a little more.

"Clothes and school supplies. Have you guys had lunch?"

Tyler hooked a thumb toward the retro café. "In there. Miss Lisa sat with us and told us stories about Christmas. Baby Jesus. And why he got born in a barn."

"A barn's actually not a bad place to be born." Brett met the little guy's look of surprise with one of conviction. "Safe. Warm. Dry. Cozy. Quiet. Maybe the innkeeper was really trying to keep Mary safe from others."

"Brett." Haley put her hand along his arm and her smile said his words had an effect. And he liked having an effect on Haley Jennings. "That's a lovely way to look at it."

"I did a lot of time in the desert. Visited the Holy Land twice. Back in those days—" he jutted his chin toward the beautiful Nativity set showcased in the entryway "—it wasn't uncommon for women to deliver in a cave. Or a stable. Safety and privacy were of great importance."

"I've never thought of it like that." Haley squeezed his arm and her look, her touch, her wonder at life made him feel stronger and taller. "You're sure about this?" She stroked Tyler's cheek with a gentle hand, a hand born to mother, in Brett's unskilled opinion. And something in her gentle stroke made him long for a second chance to father someone. A chance to do it right, from beginning to end.

"Absolutely. We'll meet you for supper tonight over at the Crossroads. And I'll pick up some dessert at the Angelica Sweet Shop."

"And cookies from the cookie store?" Todd lifted hopeful eyes to Brett's.

"The Colonial Cookie Kitchen has just now been declared stop number one," Brett assured him. "And if you guys are good while we shop, I'll have a treat for you later. But no whining."

"And we better watch out. We better not cry." Tyler slanted a serious look Brett's way, underscoring his verbal reminder that Christmas was coming.

"We better not pout," Todd added, not to be outdone.

"Exactly." Brett leveled a firm look at both boys, then a gentler one at Haley. "Good luck with all this." He encompassed the co-op in a gaze before resettling it on her. "Although I'm sure you've got it well in hand."

She offered a grim smile. "You can count on it."

He knew he could. He also knew she'd have had everything in tip-top shape if she hadn't taken on the care of these two little boys, but she'd taken that leap of faith despite the risk to her new business and bankbook. That devotion inspired him to do the same.

* * *

Lisa Fitzgerald curtailed Haley as she aimed for the office to send out an urgent vendor email. "It didn't go well, I take it?"

"About as far from well as you can get." Haley waved an aggravated hand around. "And it's not like we didn't know he was coming. Or that I didn't send out a memo Saturday and Sunday to remind people to prepare for his inspection."

"I know." Lisa sent her a sympathetic look. "Sales were good and people got tired. And a little greedy." She let her gaze slide left, indicating one of the cited displays. "Space and sales at Christmas are crucial to some vendors."

"But not at the cost of being fined or shut down. Or what if there was a fire or a natural disaster? And people couldn't access the exit doors or windows?" Haley swept the sprawling old factory room a focused look. "We've got false walls, overhead lighting, decorative things strung everywhere, all according to code. There's no reason to break code to make a few extra bucks."

"You and I are in full agreement." Lisa stepped closer and flashed Haley a look of understanding. "But that's because we've had to do battle in our lives. Some folks don't get that."

Haley knew what she meant. Lisa was a breast cancer survivor. She won her life and lost her husband, a man who couldn't stay the course to fight off a debilitating and sometimes deadly disease with his wife.

Alone, Lisa had made it her mission to educate people through Gardens and Greens, the family garden store she ran for her parents. Her philanthropy touched people throughout Allegany County.

Folks would drive an extra ten miles or ten minutes to shop at Lisa's place. Having her do a second location in the co-op was a coup for Haley because Lisa Fitzgerald drew business like flies to honey. Only way nicer. They'd already planned a Pink Ribbon celebration as part of the co-op's February romance theme, and Lisa had an all-out extravaganza at the family farm garden shop in May, a pink salute to summer, warmth, gardens and breast cancer patients everywhere.

"I'm emailing everyone for an emergency meeting. We'll have this in shape by Thursday—"

"Good timing." Lisa nodded firmly. "Quick, and before the weekend."

"Exactly. And in the meantime, I'm fixing what I can myself."

Lisa frowned. "Shouldn't we make the responsible vendors do that?"

"In a perfect world, yes." Haley started for the stairs, determined. "But it's slow today, and I've got the gift of time because Brett's got the boys."

She didn't miss Lisa's interested upturned brow, but chose to ignore it and move on. "And my bank draft is tied up until this inspection comes out clean. Which means I can't pay people until this gets done."

"Oh, Haley." Lisa moved forward, concerned. "I had no idea. Why didn't you say something?"

"Because running the place is my job." Haley met her gaze frankly. "And I don't want people thinking I'm too young or inexperienced to do it right. So I kept this to myself thinking it was the right thing to do, only now I've got contractors waiting in line for a payment they expected two weeks ago. And that's beyond embarrassing."

"I'll help." Lisa rolled up the sleeves of her turtleneck and fell into step with Haley. "We'll tackle the upstairs first and work our way down. The front's covered until closing, so we're good to go."

"Lisa." Haley paused and met Lisa's look. "You don't have to do this."

"I do," the taller woman argued. "Christmas tree business is traditionally slow on Mondays, my brother and his wife are overseeing things at the farm so Dad can take care of Mom and having an indoor site to sell greens is a perfect way to round things out. I'm totally determined that this cooperative will not only succeed but thrive. And I love keeping busy."

And then some, but because Haley reflected that ambition, it was nice to have a comrade, ready to do whatever it took to get things done. "Then let's go."

"Lead the way."

Some of Haley's frustration eased. Knowing the boys were in good hands, and that she had help at Bennington Station, calmed the tingle of worry snaking along her spine. If she could just get through the madness of Christmas, she'd be fine. Just fine.

Chapter Seven

Brett learned two very important lessons on his impromptu shopping trip. First, that no sane adult should take two kids shopping with less than a one-to-one ratio of adult to child and he was one adult short.

Second? Shopping with kids was exhausting.

Who knew that one little boy could disappear into a rack of women's clothing so effectively? And stay that quiet?

Covert ops had nothing on shopping with Todd and Tyler.

"Brett, I'm hungry. Can we stop now?"

"We've found only coats and hats. We need a bunch more stuff, bud."

Tyler frowned. Todd rubbed his eyes.

Nap time.

He hadn't thought of that. Tyler would be okay if needed, but Todd? The little guy needed a nap. Or he'd be falling asleep under some rack-to-floor dress display and they'd never find him without an Amber Alert.

"And I've got to go."

"Go?" Brett noted the worried look on Todd's face. Understanding dawned. "Oh. Go. Gotcha. There's a men's room in the back corner."

"We can't go alone." Tyler looked up at him as if he'd grown two heads, minimal.

"We might get pidnapped," Todd explained earnestly.

Brett couldn't have that, right? "Let's go, men." He ushered them into the men's bathroom, coached them on washing their hands and by the time they were done, Todd looked less worried. Another lesson learned.

"How about this?" Brett held up the two warm coats, snowpants, hats and mittens they'd selected. "What if we find boots today, and tomorrow we can shop for regular clothes? That way we can spread out the fun."

Tyler tucked his little hand into Brett's. "I would like that. A lot. I was always wishing I'd get new clothes, Brett."

Todd nodded. "Me, too. Like a superhero shirt. And some running shoes so I can run fast, fast, fast."

Brett's heart melted. The rusted tangle of chains fell a little more to the side as the boys gazed up at him. "Okay, boots today. Then ice cream."

The boys beamed, excited.

"And then naps with Derringer."

"I fink I wuv him," Todd exclaimed.

"*Th*ink." Brett stressed the opening sound, having heard Haley and LuAnn do the same thing.

Todd nodded and grinned. "F-f-f-ink!"

"You're getting there, kid." He grabbed Todd's hand. By the time they got the boots fitted and ate mini-sundaes at Colonial Cookie Kitchen's ice-cream parlor, it was four o'clock. The perfect time for a quick nap.

Only Todd wasn't tired. Just ornery.

And Tyler wanted to play with the trains. Not sleep.

Too late, Brett realized they'd gotten their second wind and naps were a no-go. Another lesson learned, albeit too late for today and Haley would have her hands full tonight.

He'd commanded legions of armed fighting men with more acuity than he showed leading two little boys around a department store, but they'd survived. That was good, right?

He fed the boys and called Haley on her cell phone.

"Brett, hey. What's up? Are the boys okay? I was just ducking out of here and heading your way."

"Don't," he told her. "I'll meet you at your apartment. I've got food and two tired boys who probably want a seven o'clock bedtime whether they know it or not."

Haley's laugh was just what he needed to hear. "I might just join them. Okay, I'm leaving here now and I'll be home in two minutes."

"I'm on my way."

She met him at the door and he didn't pretend the joy he felt seeing her. It flooded him, a wash of emotional peace, the kind of feeling a man would like to come home to every day. And every night. "Special delivery."

She laughed and accepted the to-go container of food. "I'm starved, so this is most welcome."

"And these." He handed in plastic bags of boys' outerwear.

"Oh, Brett, I can't wait to see them." Her grin inspired his.

"And here we have…" He ushered the boys into the apartment and realized the whole setting was pretty sparse. Not like Haley at all. Bare walls, a pale rug, scant furniture. "Two tired boys."

"I'm not tired." Tyler scowled and scrubbed a toe into the rug. "He is. And he started it."

"Did not!"

"Did, too!"

"I'm finishing it." Brett used his army voice. It did the trick. Both boys went quiet, but the scowls remained intact. "Hang up your coats, put your shoes away and go get pajamas on."

"I wanna see TV!"

"Me, too!"

"You're not the boss of me!"

"I want my mommy!"

Brett edged closer to Haley. "I say we divide and conquer."

"I agree. I've got Todd."

"Then I'm all over Tyler."

He didn't have time to appreciate her smile of agreement. He scooped Tyler up, wrestled him around and noogied his head while she got Todd ready in the bedroom beyond.

A pair of pajamas came flying out the door.

Brett helped the sullen little guy into them.

The sound of water being shut off meant Todd had brushed his teeth.

He exchanged places with Haley and watched as Tyler pretended to brush his teeth. Was it worth a fight tonight, knowing he'd messed up their earlier rest time?

No.

But he'd be smarter tomorrow.

By the time they'd read two stories and gotten the boys settled, he was contemplating joining a gym to get himself back into top shape because keeping up with two busy boys wasn't a given.

"Whew. Done. And we lived to tell the tale." Haley high-fived him, grinned and dropped into the lone chair in the room. "Now if they actually fall asleep…"

"You mean they might not?"

She sent him a look that said "Get real, pal." "They may. They may not. Show me what you bought."

It seemed meager from the amount of time he'd spent, but Haley ooohed and aahed over the coats, snow pants and accessories like he was the greatest man on Earth. And her enthusiasm made him feel that way. "I love that they're the same color scheme, but not the same jackets," she told him. "And that shade of blue looks good on both boys."

"I agree. And now—" he sat back and leveled her a straight-on gaze "—we need to talk."

"O-kay." The way she drew out the word said she

wondered where he was headed. Her bottom teeth grabbed her upper lip, a habit when she grew concerned. "About the fire inspection today?"

He shook his head. "No, I figured you were all over that list the minute I walked out the door with the boys."

Her look said he was spot on, but he already knew that. Haley wasn't exactly the type to let grass grow beneath her feet. "No, I want to talk about the boys' schedules."

"Nonexistent at the moment." She offered the words and the look of worry deepened.

"I think we can fix that," he told her.

"I don't see how until I've got the medical and legal papers done."

"I want to help with those."

She frowned, ready to wave him off, but he refused to be put off, a soldier's trait that held him in good stead. "I've got time. You don't. I've got two inspections Wednesday, then yours on Thursday, but that's it until after the first of the year and Bud Schmidt, the regular fire inspector, might be back on the job by then. LuAnn has already offered to watch the boys Wednesday, and Charlie's offered to take them to see Bwana Jim so I can get the medical and legal records worked out."

"I can't let you do all that." Haley frowned and inched forward. "I appreciate all this, Brett, but it isn't your job, your responsibility. It's just come at an awful time for me, with a new business venture just opening up—"

"Exactly why I should do it." He decided to explain without explaining fully. At some point in time, they could swap stories and maybe she wouldn't think he was a deadbeat dad. But right now, he knew he could and should help. End of story. "I've got the time. Charlie and LuAnn are back at the store. Les is feeling better and will be back for the weekend. My stint in the army taught me how to get around red tape, Haley, and that's what we need to settle the boys in properly."

"I agree with all that." She said the words slowly, as if reluctant to continue. She paused, took a deep breath, then met his gaze straight on, a trait he admired. "But these guys have lost a lot, Brett. Father, mother. You heard Tyler last night. He feels like he's got no home. No place to call his own. What if you do all this nice stuff, and then disappear from their lives? That can't be good for them, right?"

He couldn't fault her logic, but... "Haley, my home and business are across the street. Logistics say I'm not going anywhere. Unless..." He smiled and got to his feet, then crossed the room. She rose, too, uncertain, but looking way too wonderful for him to mess up this second chance. "You're worried about this." He waved a hand between them, his gaze implying the growing attraction.

She read his inference and her mouth, soft and sweet, curved in a small smile.

Could he imagine this feeling growing? Evolving into something life-altering?

Tonight he could.

Should he? Maybe not. Maybe he didn't deserve a second chance to be a good father.

But on the other hand, God was the God of second chances. He blessed atonement. He offered forgiveness freely, and Brett had begged forgiveness more than once.

His phone buzzed, interrupting the moment, but he eased back, not wanting to break the conversation, knowing he needed to check the number.

His mother.

Duty called.

He waved the phone and offered a look of apology. "Gotta go. It's my mother."

"Of course." She acquiesced as if motherly respect should be a given. If only that was true.

And the fact that he didn't want to leave?

Bittersweet but wondrous, and Brett couldn't remember the last time he'd seen life as wondrous. It felt good. Mighty good. He held on to that emotion as he headed out the door, never sure what a phone call from his mother might bring. But tonight?

He felt like he could handle anything that came his way.

Chapter Eight

Brett opened the door to his little house before Haley had the boys out of the car the next morning. His anticipation made her feel like she could do anything.

His smile? Ditto.

The way his gaze rested on her face, as if wondering when he might kiss her?

That brought heat to her cheeks and she had to school herself to calm things down. Take this slow. Think of the boys. Sending them the wrong message could be harmful. She might not have been prepared for this sudden bend in the road, but she had every intention of doing it right. As much as she could, anyway. And once she got through the craziness of the holiday season, she'd be good to go.

She hoped.

"This rain is annoying." Brett sent the sky a quick look as the boys trooped into the house.

"And then some. I'd much rather have snow." Haley watched as he shrugged into his bomber jacket over an ivory-and-tan heathered sweater. He looked amazing. Strong. Vigorous. He sent her a quick grin.

"Do I pass inspection?"

She blushed but refused to waffle. "I'd go straight to heart-stopping, but I might be a little over-the-top."

His chuckle made her smile inside and out, the sound filled with hope and promise and all things good. He glanced at his watch, then nodded across the street as they shifted the boys' car seats into his SUV. "Are you sure you can't leave for a few hours and join us? I figured we'd go straight to Olean, shop for a couple of hours, head back here and have lunch, then naps. While they're napping I'm going to make calls about the legal and medical stuff. See if we can get that straightened around."

She'd love to. To spend the morning shopping with Brett and the boys would be fun.

But there were only twenty-seven shopping days until Christmas. As owner and manager of a fledgling business, that meant she had twenty-seven days of work. She shook her head. Her refusal put a niggle of concern in Brett's eye, but he accepted her rebuttal with an easy nod.

"Hey, how did your phone call with your mother go last night?" She helped Todd adjust his buckles and then tested them for a good fit. Perfect.

"Fine." Brett gave Tyler a high-five for getting himself strapped into the booster seat and came around the hood. "She needed a ride to an early AA meeting this morning."

His honesty didn't surprise her. It made her feel good actually, knowing he could and would talk about things. She'd lived a life rife with family secrets. Facts treated as fiction. Problems swept aside with the stroke of a pen on a check. She'd vowed to never live her life that way. "Are you picking her up now?"

"Already did it. She was going to the early morning session, then on for coffee and fellowship. If she needs a ride back home, she'll call me later." He winked at Todd and that made the little guy giggle in his seat. "He likes sitting up high in the SUV."

"They love it." Haley made a face and scanned her car. "At some point I'll have to go more family-friendly, but I'm skating my way through the holidays right now. You understand."

He brought a hand up to her face. Cupped her cheek. His smile said he understood, but something in his eyes, his gaze said he wished he didn't. "I've finally learned that Christmas with children isn't something to ever be taken lightly."

His words stung.

He didn't mean them to. She saw that. And the broad hand against her cheek said he was offering simple advice, not an edict.

But this timing wasn't of her doing and she had four dozen vendors who'd staked time and money to make Bennington Station a success. She couldn't turn her back on them. And she couldn't turn her back on the boys. Balance. It was all about balance.

"I'll see you later." He released her cheek with a

gentle smile. A smile that said he didn't want to corner her or make her feel guilty. So why did she feel both?

"Okay. And Brett?"

"Yes?" He turned as he settled himself into the driver's seat of the big, rangy SUV.

"Thank you. For everything."

His smile deepened. "Get in your car. You're getting wet. I'll see you later. You've got my cell number in your phone, right?"

"On speed dial."

"Good girl."

Haley almost preened under his approval and then wondered if she was being ridiculous. Maybe, but it was the best feeling she'd ever had. She hopped into the convertible and took the two-minute drive over to the co-op.

Lisa Fitzgerald met her inside. "We made significant progress yesterday."

"We did." Haley hung up her coat and scarf in the office and headed for the east wing of shops. "And if we get the east wing scoured and adjusted today, we're good for Thursday's inspection."

"And that bank draft."

"Amen." She withdrew Brett's list of citations from her desk and handed it to Lisa. "Would you just double check and make sure I've covered everything noted on the second floor?"

"I'm on it."

Lisa found Haley near the checkout area about

twenty minutes later and handed off the sheet, smiling. "Done. Perfect. Stellar."

"Good." Haley set up the cash drawer for the day, glanced around and then dropped her attention to the pink sheet in her hand. "I'll get started on this. We've got six vendors on site today. I scheduled ten for tomorrow because we've got several bus tours coming down from Rochester and Buffalo."

"Awesome. I love it when the buses pull up."

"It still amazes me," Haley admitted. "I look around, I see how close we are to being complete with the new showroom done for spring and summer sales, with the factory side done for this Christmas, and I'm continually surprised that it's moving so quickly."

"You came to town with a good plan, great numbers and real estate backing." Lisa shrugged. "All conduits of good business, Haley."

"Thank you." She smiled at Lisa and started toward the eastern end of the co-op layout.

"Who's got the boys?"

Haley swung back. "Brett's taking them shopping for clothes in Olean."

"Now?"

Haley nodded. "The stores open at nine because of the Christmas season, so he's heading out early."

"Why are you here?"

Haley frowned and took a step back toward Lisa. "Because I'm working here."

"It's Tuesday." Lisa folded her arms and sent Haley a commonsense look. "We've got plenty of help on hand, I can fix anything on the east side that needs attention for the fire inspection, and you should be shopping with those boys."

"It's not that easy," Haley began, but Lisa interrupted by grabbing the pink sheet back out of Haley's hand.

"Yes, it is. Stop being stubborn. You know I'll do this and do it right. If you're back by this afternoon, we can double check things together, and we're open until eight tonight, so when did you think you were going to see those boys?"

Guilt power punched her. She'd figured she wouldn't see the boys and Brett's look that morning had underscored her misgivings. "You're all right here?"

"Yes." Lisa made a face like that was a given.

Haley hesitated, then confessed, "It's hard to not feel guilty this week. I'm either cutting the boys short or the business short. There doesn't seem to be a happy medium."

"We'll find one," Lisa promised. She gave Haley a half hug. "If nothing else, having cancer taught me to celebrate life. Grasp the moment. Live for tomorrow but enjoy today. If it was crucial for you to be here today, I'd agree." She stepped back. "But it's Tuesday and shopping with kids is best done with as many adults as possible. Go." She pointed toward Haley's office. "Grab your coat and get out of here. Have fun with the boys in your life."

She didn't mention Brett's name, but Haley knew exactly what she meant. She grinned, strode into her tiny office, grabbed her stuff and headed for the door. "Thank you, Lisa."

"Don't mention it." Lisa headed east while Haley moved north. "Just remember that the word *cooperative* means we're all in it together. You might own it—" she fist-pumped a hand in solidarity "—but we've all got a stake in its success."

Haley recognized the truth in Lisa's words. How had she forgotten that?

Because not all vendors are as focused and trustworthy as Lisa, her conscience reminded her. *Otherwise you wouldn't have failed that first inspection.*

Know your people.

Professors hammered that point in her business classes and she should have paid closer attention to the advice. Her Pollyanna mind-set wanted everyone to be happy and work hard. The real world said only twenty-five percent of workers would fall in that range.

Now she needed to more accurately assess that twenty-five percent and deputize them.

That phrase made her smile as she started the car and aimed for I-86. She mentally kicked herself for not seeing the common sense of this sooner. Mornings weren't as busy and helping with the boys should be her primary responsibility.

She headed west, found a Christmas music radio station and let herself relax into the true reason for the season.

Why did she allow other things to mute the holiness of the season? She'd try to do better, she promised herself in the half-hour ride. And she'd count on Lisa and Brett to remind her to do just that.

"Hey, miss us already?" Brett answered the call as he and the boys headed for the kids' clothing department. "I did invite you along, remember?"

"Where are you?"

"Penney's. Why?"

"Which department?"

"Um…" He glanced around and frowned. "Heading through socks and up to children's clothing."

"See you in five."

"What?"

But she'd hung up. He turned, scanned the thin number of shoppers for an early Tuesday in late November and wondered if he'd heard right. She was here? Ready to shop with them?

Or had something gone wrong? His heart went straight to overdrive, wondering.

"What's wrong, Brett?"

Oops. Tyler's oversensitive nature had picked up his vibes. He had to remember that the five-year-old tuned into things with great acuity. He didn't know if all kids were like that, or if Tyler's life had thrust that awareness on him at too early an age, but he'd have to watch his reactions around the little guy. "Nothing, bud. I think Aunt Haley's going to join us after all."

"Really?" Todd's smile widened from the circle of Brett's arm. "I fink I will wuv that a wot!"

"A l-l-lot," said a familiar voice behind them,

stressing the *L* sound. "Remember, Todd? Practice la-la-la-la-la."

"Aunt Haley!"

"You came!"

"Oh, I'm so glad you did!"

"Me, too." Brett turned at the top of the escalator and met her gaze, grinning like a schoolboy and unashamed to admit it. "How did you pull yourself free?"

"Lisa Fitzgerald reminded me that Tuesdays are slow, she's perfectly capable of fixing the citation items we couldn't get done yesterday and that I need to learn to delegate."

"She's one smart lady."

"Like Aunt Haley?" Tyler asked the question as Haley bent to plant butterfly kisses along his cheek. He rubbed them away but grinned.

"Yes." Brett smiled at her, glanced at her mouth with a hint of longing, then winked. "Boys' clothes. Front and center."

She took Tyler's hand and led the way, but didn't pretend to miss the flirtation. Her eyes and smile confirmed the shared feeling, making Brett wonder if this was truly happening.

Hadn't he been fairly down in the dumps just a week ago?

And now…

He didn't bother finishing the thought because Todd was grabbing shirts with superhero motifs while Tyler was wriggling over a lined athletic zip-up jacket complete with Diego, the Animal Rescuer.

"Should we try things on?" He directed the question at Haley and was glad when her look reflected his confusion.

"I have no idea. How about if we try the first things on for size, and then just shop in the same size range?"

"Sounds good to me." He took the boys by the hand and headed into the changing area. "You scout things out while we get into this stuff."

"Tag-team approach." She held two pairs of camouflage pants aloft. "I'm on it."

She'd joined them.

Brett's heart opened a little more having her here. Neither of them knew a thing about buying kids' clothes or raising little boys, but together...

The thought of together with Haley broadened his smile. Lightened his step.

Maybe together they could make a difference in two little lives that had lost so much.

"We need food." Haley surveyed the mess of bags and squatted to Tyler's level a couple of hours later. "And you get to pick because you were such a big help with your little brother."

His grin made her smile.

He longed to be cared for. Cherished. Loved. Who didn't?

The thought of losing both parents at such a fragile age stymied her. Lisa's words of wisdom reminded her to live in the day, the moment. But that was easier said than done sometimes. And when she got involved in co-op business, she sometimes forgot the boys altogether.

That couldn't possibly be normal, could it?

"Can we have hot dogs today?"

"Absolutely. We've got some of the best hot dogs around at the Texas Hot back in Wellsville." Brett unlocked the SUV and helped Haley stow the bags into the rear of the car. "Hey, you. Watch it." He grabbed Todd as the three-year-old darted toward the street. "Bud, that's dangerous. We never go into the street without a grown-up holding our hand, okay?"

"Okay."

Todd nodded, sincere, but he'd dashed across Brett's small parking lot twice in the past few days. The thought of anything happening to him toughened Haley's voice. "We're serious, Todd." She moved closer, but it was hard to be firm with the little guy. His eyes went wide and round. His lip quivered. His chin followed suit and his cheeks puffed, ready to storm. She stretched and kissed his cheek. "We love you, little dude. We don't want anything to happen to you and streets are dangerous."

"And parking lots," Tyler offered.

"Exactly," Haley confirmed. "Any place that cars go is dangerous to kids. We want you safe. Okay?"

He nodded, but the crumpled look lingered.

Haley turned away, ready to crumple right back, hating her role of being rough and tough when all she wanted to do was have fun with them. How did parents do this stuff? How did they cope with woebegone faces and raw emotions?

Brett shoulder-nudged her. "You realize kids are the world's greatest natural actors, right? And that the whole world's a stage? And you just got played?"

"But…"

"No buts. Don't let the meekness fool you. My guess is we don't dare let down our guard where Todd is concerned. He has no sense of danger."

"Is that normal?"

"My brother Ben was like that." His face went quiet, remembering. "He'd grab hold of something and jump in, then figure out an escape route later."

"Whereas you have your routes preplanned and a backup exit, just in case."

Her words chased the stillness away. "That kept me in good stead with Uncle Sam for a long time. Plan your work. Work your plan."

"I can't argue because that's a good philosophy." She sent a quick look to Todd. "But he breaks my heart when he does that whole lip-shudder thing. I want to make it all better."

"Yeah, it's quite effective. I think they come with that preprogrammed."

"Which means I'm too soft," Haley interjected.

"Just soft enough, I'd say." Brett grinned, tweaked her scarf and climbed into the SUV. "See you in Wellsville."

"I have to get back to the co-op." Haley pulled out her phone and grimaced. "But I had fun with you guys this morning."

"You need to eat."

"Granola bar. And yogurt. Yum."

He scowled, but then shrugged. "Okay. I'll take the boys over to your place later so they can be ready for bed when you close up."

"Thanks, Brett."

"None needed. See you later."

"Will do." She waved and crossed the road to the parking lot. They'd had a good morning. Productive. And she'd pay Brett back for the clothing once her draft cleared her account, but he was right. The boys needed things now. Snow was predicted by the week's end, and they had to be prepared.

So did she.

A snowy weekend could slow sales, so businesses had to be on top of their game every day. Lost weekend sales before Christmas could never be regained, and she'd seen that first-hand in Pennsylvania. But hard work and pre-weekend sale incentives were her mainstay for the next four weeks. Preparations made for good business, and Haley took that ethic seriously, because a bottom line in the black when all is said and done?

That was the goal of any good business owner.

Chapter Nine

Brett's cell phone buzzed him as he tucked Todd into the car seat after lunch. For kids who professed to love only chicken nuggets, the boys made short work of the famous Wellsville hot dogs. He checked Todd's closure to make sure it clicked as he grappled the phone. "Brett Stanton."

"I know who you are." A thin giggle followed the words, the hint of slur telling Brett more than he wanted to know.

"Mom?"

"I know who I am, too." Again the giggle, louder this time, as if she'd said something really funny. She hadn't. "I need a ride, son."

He'd figured that out the minute he heard the drawl of her words. The silly giggle. But he had the boys with him. Could he pick up his inebriated mother while the boys rode along in the backseat?

Did he have a choice?

"Where are you?"

"On East. At the Leaning Post."

"Are you outside?"

"Brr. No." She said it with an exaggerated shiver. "It's cold out there, Brett."

"I know." He climbed into the driver's seat, affixed his seat belt and finished the call before he pulled into the light midday traffic. "But I've got some little guys with me and I can't bring them into the bar."

"Lounge," she corrected smoothly. "Bars are unsavory places."

He wouldn't quibble. There was no reasoning with her once the alcohol took hold, and the anniversary of Ben's death loomed shortly after Christmas. She'd told him once that she couldn't face Christmas without knowing she'd face that anniversary less than a week later. Therefore, she dreaded Christmas.

"Well, the boys have to stay in the car. Can you meet me outside in five minutes, Mom? Please?"

The "please" softened her tone. "Of course I will, dear. And thank you very much for calling."

He hadn't called. She did. But something about being on the phone when drinking put her in the strangest mood, as if playing a part. Which only meant she took the drama queen mentality more to heart while drinking.

He thrust the car into gear, moved into the traffic lane and pulled parallel with the curb outside the bar a few minutes later, hoping she'd come outside.

She had. And she didn't look too bad. Tweaked, but not wasted. And Brett had enough army experience to know the difference. Men and women on leave and furlough often did very interesting things. His mother was no different. "Hey, Mom."

He exited the car, moved around front and helped her into the passenger side. "Thank you, Brett." She smiled down at him, and how he wished she'd smile like that when she was sober.

She didn't. Sober meant she had to face the world, try harder, meet her demons face-to-face. In Joanna Stanton's mixed-up world, drunk was better.

"You're welcome." He came back around the car. By the time he'd climbed into his seat, she'd noticed the boys.

"Boys?"

He nodded, grim, wondering if he'd done the right thing. "These are my two new friends. Mom, this is Tyler." Brett indicated the older boy with a thrust of his chin. "And Todd."

She turned to look at them, two little boys, all rough and tumble, dressed in camo fleece and peaceful for the moment. "Oh."

Her face softened. She sighed and a tiny smile flickered from cheek to cheek as if dancing. It faded, then grew. "Oh," she said again, her voice kind of water-soft. "Hello, boys."

Tyler took her reaction in stride. "Hello. Are you Brett's mom?"

She nodded, still staring at them. "Yes."

"I'm Todd." The three-year-old was not to be outdone. He stretched forward and reached for her hand.

"I'm free years old and I like to play wiff Brett's trains. Do you?"

His mother turned Brett's way as if she just remembered he was in the car. "You have trains, Brett?"

She never came to his place. She'd refused every invitation he'd extended. Therefore, he'd stopped offering. "Yes."

"Kids' trains?" She seemed astounded that a grown man would have toys hanging around his home. Put that way, it sounded odd to Brett, too.

"Model trains."

"Ah." She shifted further and smiled back at the boys, a genuine smile, the kind Brett longed for all his life. "Brett always liked to play with trains."

He hadn't. He'd never owned a train. He swallowed a sigh and said, "You might be thinking of Ben. I never had trains. Maybe he did."

"Ben's gone."

Brett's heart twisted. Drinking slurred more than her tongue. It melded memories out of place, out of time. "I meant when he was little."

"There was hardly money for food, much less trains." She began to look upset. Misgiving grew in Brett's chest. She didn't like to be wrong when she was drinking. Or corrected. Or reminded. The three conditions made discussions fairly easy and mundane as long as the topic remained inane.

Brett continued to drive, wishing the miles away. He shouldn't have picked her up in her condition, not with the boys in the car. He should have—

"My name is Joanna." She'd turned again, and something in her voice, the tilt of her head, caught Brett by surprise. "Joanna Stanton. What's yours?"

"Tyler." Tyler didn't seem to think it was odd that Brett had already introduced them. He reached out and grasped the fingers she extended. "Tyler Jennings."

"And you, sir?" She held out a very polite hand to Todd. He giggled before stretching forward. "I'm still Todd." He burst out laughing as if she was the funniest thing he'd ever seen or heard, and Brett knew a moment of ultimate fear.

Would she misconstrue his childish antics and think he was laughing at her?

Brett hoped not. Drinking heightened her anxiety and depression and it didn't take much to tip her over the edge into mania. How he wished…

But wishing was of little use. He'd wished before, praying she'd stop drinking. Just be a mom. It hadn't happened until three years after he'd gone into the army, and then she'd started drinking again three years before he retired. Once Ben died.

Obviously three was not his good luck number.

Joanna took no offense, an answer to Brett's prayer. "Of course you are," she exclaimed. She smiled at Todd's little face, and Brett sensed a glimmer of the mother he knew as a small child. Kind. Sweet. Loving.

He missed her.

He pulled into the parking lot of her complex, circled around to her apartment building, then parked. He started to climb out, but she waved him back in. "Don't leave those boys," she chastised. She held up a set of keys, almost as if she was sober. "I can let myself in."

She could, but Brett had always thought it right to walk a lady to the door. This lady happened to be his mother, but it was still the right thing to do. He started to ignore her advice, but she hurried forward, thwarting him. "Stay there. Take care of those precious boys. I'll call you tomorrow."

"Okay," he said, wondering what she meant. She never called him unless she needed a ride. Her car had been seized two years before, but that was a good thing, Brett decided. His mother didn't have the sense to not drink and drive, so losing the car back to the bank was a blessing in disguise. She couldn't crash a car she didn't have. He watched her as she applied her key and let herself into the first level of the building. When she made it into her apartment, she came to the front window and waved.

And while she waved, she smiled. She looked almost…happy. Invigorated.

Todd waved back, his round cheeks rose-red from the wind and chill. Tyler offered a meeker variety, but his eyes sparkled with something that hadn't been there minutes before. It struck Brett like a ton of bricks as he drove away.

They liked his mother. They connected.

And in some way, they seemed good for her. As if their presence made her push to be more normal.

Brett had been fooled in the past. When it came to his mother, he was the doubting disciple, a true

Thomas. He'd been let down too many times to put much credence in a ten-minute ride.

And yet…

Something in her face. Her gaze. The way she rested her look on those boys, as if they meant something. Something good and pure and holy.

It was a look Brett had longed for growing up. A look that disappeared after his father had left and the drinking began. A look that meant someone cared about him.

Most likely he'd imagined it.

"I like her." Todd yawned around the words, his sleepy eyes drifting closed. "She's nice, Bwett. Like you."

Tyler put a finger to his lips, warning Brett that Todd was falling asleep. And if the look on Tyler's face meant anything, Brett figured he'd snuggle up alongside the big red dog and doze off, too. Brett intended to use the quiet time to make some phone calls and figure out how to get the legal and medical technicalities straightened out for Haley. He saw the worry in her face. He understood the lack of time. But a part of him wished she could sit back and relax a little. Enjoy this blessed time with the boys.

If helping her resulted in less worry and more time for the kids, Brett was more than willing to expend the effort.

"Brett?"

LuAnn's cheerful voice hailed him from the storefront as he climbed out of the car a few minutes later. He put a finger to his lips, then pointed into the SUV.

She smiled her understanding when Tyler jumped down from the passenger side. "Ah. Passengers."

Brett bundled Todd into his arms, trying not to jostle him too much. "LuAnn, can you?" He nodded toward the bungalow.

"I can indeed!" She bustled across the driveway separating his house from the corner store and plied a key from the ring she kept in her pocket. She pushed the door open.

Derringer met them, tail wagging, tongue lolling, about as much effort as the old boy had expended in the past year.

The boys, Brett realized. Their invigorating effect was working on him and the dog.

LuAnn echoed his thoughts. "He's got a new lease on life, having these boys around, Brett. He's always loved kids. Why, just look at him!"

The trusty dog lapped Tyler's face with a big, wet tongue before he eased out the door and into the yard for a quick walk around.

"Can I go out with Derringer?" Tyler asked.

"Not right now." Brett whispered the answer, loath to wake Todd. "Let me put—"

"I'll take him out with me," LuAnn insisted. "We'll keep an eye on Derringer together."

"Thanks." Tyler grinned up at her and Brett's heart moved once more. Tyler didn't smile a lot, and when he did, the look was sheltered. Hesitant.

Not now. As he walked back outside with LuAnn, the rain didn't seem to bother him or the dog. They seemed content to get wet together.

Eight thirty-five.

The old country clock cemented Haley's growing load of guilt as she locked up the co-op.

Brett had cared for the boys all day. He'd shopped with them, fed them, given them naps and rushed Todd to the bathroom most likely.

And he did it all with nothing in it for him.

Haley had never met a man like Brett. Giving. Trusting. Funny. Solid.

Her father was the anti-Brett. Weak. Self-absorbed. An excuse maker with multiple families in as many states. Her stepfather was a successful businessman in Olean, New York, but an appearances-only kind of guy. That made him a perfect fit for her mother.

Her brother, Anthony, had been like Brett but she'd been too young to appreciate his qualities the few times they'd met. Maybe having Brett around was God's way of easing the boys through their losses. A strong, focused man like their father to offset the entrepreneur with no time to care for them.

Grim, she hurried up the steps to her bare-bones apartment.

"Shh." Brett put a finger to his mouth as she burst through the door, as if ten seconds would make a difference when she'd been gone all day.

"Oh. Sorry." She shut the door with a quiet squeak

and click before she peeled off her coat and scarf. "They're in bed?"

"Just."

"Ah." He must have read her look of disappointment, but he wasn't the type to mollycoddle. She'd figured that out the first day. Comfort, yes. Spoil? No.

"They had a good day." He kept his voice soft as she plunked into the chair opposite him. "They devoured their lunch, so we can add hot dogs to the list of desirable foods. We tried stew for supper and we can put that in the column labeled dismal failure. I ended up substituting P.B. and J."

"No stew. Check!"

He smiled. "They love chocolate milk, apple juice, drink boxes and my mother."

"Your mother?" Haley settled back. The warmth and comfort of the wide-backed chair wrapped around her, easing the frenzied pace she'd kept up all day. "They got to meet your mother before I did? How is that fair?"

He acknowledged the teasing with the crooked smile she'd spotted on Thanksgiving, then huffed a breath. "She was drunk, Haley."

Haley shifted forward, concerned. "But she went to AA this morning, right?"

He looked as confused as she felt, but how much harder this had to be for him because it was his mother they were talking about. Not an abstract. Not a theory. "Is this her norm, Brett? Pretending to conquer the addiction and then giving in?"

"Yes. It's worse at holiday time. And then it gets bad at Memorial Day. Fourth of July. Oh, wait, throw in Easter. And Veterans Day."

"Aw, Brett." She made a noise of commiseration. "I'm sorry."

He shrugged it off, but she saw the shaded pain in his eyes. Heard it in the matter-of-factness of his voice. Acute problems tended to solve themselves with treatment. Chronic ones?

Haley knew better. Her father's "love 'em and leave 'em" mind-set left three separate kids from three different unions, none of whom he supported or visited. Someplace in Georgia was a nineteen-year-old half sister, a young woman Haley hadn't even met. Her father refused to try harder, despite how she wished him different.

Brett was in the same boat, only with alcohol involved.

"She wasn't real bad today." He stood and put on his coat. "And it was kind of weird."

"Because?"

A thoughtful look replaced the pain. "I think she liked the boys."

"Really?" Haley smiled. "Were they behaving?"

"Yes, but it was more than that. It was like…" He moved toward the door. "Like she connected with them. She hasn't connected well with anyone since my brother Ben died."

"Oh, Brett." Haley crossed to his side. Took his hand. "I'm so sorry. When did you lose him?"

"Nearly six years ago. He was on a training exercise in Northern California. Special Forces. Chopper went down. There were no survivors." He didn't look comfortable with the short report. As if talking about his brother's death was unspoken territory.

"Brett." She drew his hand up to her face and pressed her cheek against his cool skin. "I don't know what to say. Sorry doesn't begin to cover it."

"Thank you, Haley." He stroked one finger of their clasped hands along her cheek. His touch said he appreciated her caring even if the words seemed overdone. "On another note." He pulled his hand free and zipped his coat. "I was able to contact a local pediatrician today. If we can't locate the boys' shot records we can either do a blood test to see if they have the antibodies proving they've been vaccinated or we have the vaccines redone."

"Is that dangerous? To vaccinate twice?"

"Not according to the doctor I spoke with," he assured her. "The lab tests are expensive, but there's no risk involved. They just draw blood. I spoke with Anthony's C.O. to see if they were treated on the base, but they weren't. So he has no idea what doctor they might have gone to in New Jersey."

"I see." She weighed the information, then asked, "Can I even take them to a doctor without proof of guardianship?"

"We'll find that out tomorrow. The Surrogate Court clerk will get back to us about setting a date for a hearing. You've got a copy of Anthony's will?"

"Yes. And the boys' birth certificates. And copies of—" she grimaced as she added the rest "—Anthony and Angi's death certificates."

"As hard as that is, it's good."

His tone complimented and comforted her.

"It just made sense to get them when I was in New Jersey the day before Thanksgiving," she explained. "Angi's Aunt Dell couldn't find a thing. And the boys were driving her crazy. I figured I was lucky to get what I did and get out alive."

"Boys will be boys." He grinned down at her, but then the smile softened. Stilled. His eyes dropped to her mouth for a brief moment, as if he found her lips fascinating.

She took a half step closer in silent permission.

Would he? Wouldn't he?

Oh, he did.

His arms wrapped around her and for the first time in her life Haley felt embraced. One big, brawny hand cradled the back of her head while the other held her close. His kiss started slow. Soft. Easy.

And then he deepened the kiss. The scent of kids' shampoo and coffee made her think of homes with warm fires burning. Rocking chairs. Twinkle lights on a merry Christmas tree. All things she swore she'd never have because the men in her life weren't in it for the happily ever after she desired.

Grandpa had been, but that was two generations removed. Haley thought his kind had gone extinct, but she realized otherwise while kissing Brett Stanton.

"Hey." Brett whispered the word against her cheek, her hair.

"Hmm?"

"I, um…"

"Didn't mean for that to happen?"

"Oh, I meant for it to happen." He pulled back and she read the humor in his eyes. The laughter that seemed brighter, day by day. "I was hoping you and I were on the same page."

"It would seem so." She tilted her head back. They exchanged smiles. He bent and swept a whisper-soft kiss to her mouth, so tender. So sweet.

"But I need to head across the road, close up the store and call it a night. Charlie's taking the boys tomorrow while I do those last scheduled inspections."

"Yes, I remember. They're going to see someone named Bwana—?"

"Bwana Jim. The boys will love him. Jim and Linda do a wild animal show that travels around the country. Right up the boys' alley. And the co-op is ready for my reinspection Thursday?"

"It is."

"And the court clerk in Belmont said they'd expedite things because Tyler needs to be in school."

"Excellent." She hugged him hard, putting her gratitude into the embrace.

"You're welcome." He touched one hand to her hair, just long enough to say he understood. "See you tomorrow. Sometime. Charlie will be by first thing."

"Okay." She followed him to the door and watched

him go down the stairs. He hadn't brought his car over because that would be silly, which made her a little crazy for shifting her car around the corner as often as she did.

He turned at the base of the building. "Go inside. Lock up. Get some sleep."

"I will. I just wanted to say good-night again."

His smile proved she'd said the right thing. She'd seen the shadows of pain and remembrance in his face. The set of his shoulders, rigid and tight when he talked about Ben. About his mother.

She longed to soothe him. Show him gentleness and caring.

The kiss made her nervous, though. And excited. But right now, everything in her life was moving at break-neck speed. The cooperative, the legalities, the financing, the building, the boys…

And now, Brett.

She needed to breathe. To slow things down, but she couldn't. Time wasn't on her side, but she'd soldier on.

The phrase reminded her of Brett. That kiss. His valor. His smile. The strength that emanated from him.

Tired, she made up the couch. Tucked herself in. Prayed for the boys. For Brett. For his mother. For the sister she'd never met, a sibling she'd never played dolls with.

That would be her New Year's resolution. To find Fiona and get to know her. In her spare time.

But for now? Sleep.

Chapter Ten

The scream woke her at 1:40 a.m.

Haley jumped from the couch, and banged her shin against the coffee table.

She raced for the bedroom, heart pounding. Fear of fire made her check the door with the flat of her hand first.

Cool.

She burst through.

Tyler was curled in the corner of the bed, the side nearest the wall, his little arms wound tight around his legs. He rocked to and fro, head down, body shaking, waves of fear shuddering the pillow he clutched against his face and chest.

"Tyler. Tyler, it's okay. It's all right. I'm here."

Her voice didn't comfort him. He ducked away, closer to the wall, fearful, the pillow pressed tight against his face.

"I've got you, honey." Crooning, she crawled across

Todd to get to Tyler, amazed that Todd slept through the tumult. "I'm here. It's all right. I've got you."

She had no clue how long she sat there cuddling the boy. Her clock radio and phone were in the living room, both set to wake her in the morning. But it didn't matter. She'd snuggle there until the little fellow calmed down. Until he fell asleep. Until—

The knock on the door woke her hours later. Light filtered in, thin light, the sun blocked by thick, winter clouds.

Haley sat up with a start.

The door. Knocking. Daylight.

Charlie. Which meant it was eight o'clock and she was still in bed and the boys lay sleeping, and...

She grabbed her robe, called to the boys, flew to the door and swung it wide. Charlie's sweet face smiled back at her. He took in the situation with a glance as he walked in. "I've got the boys. I've done all this before. You go get ready for work."

Charlie Simmons, superhero.

"Thank you, Charlie!" She planted a kiss on his weathered face. He grinned and headed for the coffeemaker.

"We need to get you a timed coffeemaker," he advised while he measured. "By the time you're ready, this will be good to go."

The coffee was. The boys weren't, but Charlie grabbed an outfit for each one and herded them to the car after a quick kiss goodbye. Haley waved, rushed back inside and arrived at work with moments to spare.

"Didn't I just see you?" Lisa teased as they walked in together. "Like last night around eight o'clock? How are the boys doing? Did Brett's day go well?"

Realization hit Haley like a ton of bricks.

She hadn't even talked to Tyler about his bad dream. She'd barely said a word to the boys because she was running late, frazzled and digging for time. She left them in Charlie's capable hands, but what kind of caregiver doesn't address a child's night terrors?

The worst.

"Hey, what's wrong?"

Haley shook her head. "Rough morning. I overslept, then had to hurry around and barely acknowledged the boys. Charlie came to pick them up and I just handed them off."

"And?"

"Tyler had a bad dream last night."

"Kids do that."

Haley hooked her coat onto the oak pegs along her office wall and frowned in displeasure. "But I didn't even talk to him about it. I cuddled him and we both fell asleep so I never heard either alarm. That made this morning crazy beyond belief."

"Do you know what it was about?"

Haley shook her head.

"Ouch." Lisa looked as helpless as Haley felt. "I've got nothing. No kids, no advice. But I don't think it's unusual for kids to have bad dreams. Right?"

Haley had no clue. "We've got to take the boys to

the pediatrician once I've got guardianship papers. I'll ask them. They're experts, right?"

"'We've'?" Lisa's eyes brightened as she questioned the plural pronoun.

"I meant *I've* got to take them," Haley corrected herself.

"But you said—"

"And there must be work to do, right?" Haley planted a purposeful look on her face. "Are you prepping greens for the weekend?"

Lisa let the change of subject slide, but her knowing look said she'd ferret out more in good time. "Yes. I've got them stored in the back room downstairs. It's cold there and that keeps them fresh but out of the hands of people looking for freebies out back."

A rash of car break-ins and garage burglaries had been keeping the state troopers on their toes. A recent recommendation to keep things under lock and key didn't work as well with Christmas greenery. "What about at the farm? Have you been missing things there?"

"Not that we can see." Lisa turned toward the back stairs and slipped on fingerless gloves. "I'm doing my initial wreath wiring down there to keep the mess minimal. I can't do it at home because Mom sleeps too lightly. I'd wake her, she'd want to help and she needs to rest."

"No improvement in her prognosis?"

Lisa's expression said there wasn't. "It's progressive.

And terminal. But for now, she's holding her own and I'm just grateful for every holiday we have together."

Shame made Haley look away.

Lisa was a warrior. Everyone knew it. She fought the good fight for herself and others.

Haley barely made it through the days, seeing to this, worrying about that. And with only five years' difference in their ages, shouldn't she be more like Lisa? Stoic? Strong?

"If you need me, I'll be downstairs."

"Thanks, Lisa."

The Wednesday vendor crew arrived just then. Haley exchanged greetings with them. She read the excitement in their eyes, their voices. There were two buses due midmorning before the drivers transported their passengers to lunch at The Edge, the Langley family restaurant overlooking the valley. The later buses were lunching at Spragues' Maple Farms in nearby Portville, then coming east to shop at the co-operative and historic Jamison. The success of these day trips could determine the cooperative's bottom line. Older customers sometimes shied away from winter weather changes while driving, but they were the bulk of weekday business. Bennington Station had become a new stop on the senior bus tours and Haley didn't want anything to mess this up.

Her phone rang twenty minutes later. Charlie's number flashed on the screen. "Hey, Charlie. What's up?"

"Tyler's sick."

"Sick as in?"

"Throwing up. Fever. Glassy-eyed."

Haley's lack of experience threatened to choke her. "Should he go to a doctor? The hospital? I don't know what to do, Charlie." Confessing that made her feel inept, but when it came to the boys, the feeling had grown familiar.

"LuAnn says he just needs to rest, that there's a bug going around."

"Do you think it's flu like Les had?"

Charlie's hesitation said he wasn't sure.

"I'll come get him. Are you at your place?"

"Yes. I'll keep Todd here. He seems fine, and there's no sense exposing him any more than he's been so far, right?"

Except the boys shared the same bed. And they wrestled like young pups. Haley was pretty sure that if Todd was going to catch this bug, it was most likely in the works already and Charlie and LuAnn weren't young. She couldn't risk intentionally getting them sick. "That's nice, Charlie, but I don't want you and LuAnn catching this. You've got Jess's family to think of. I'll come get both boys."

"I'm sorry, Haley."

Charlie's disappointment reflected hers. Despite her well-laid plans, the workings of the day were once again out of her control.

"'Trust in the Lord with all your heart, and lean not on your own understanding; In all your ways acknowledge Him, and He shall direct your paths.'"

The Proverb mocked her. She did trust, but her work

ethic made it tough to walk away when so much depended on her presence. Good sales. Strong rapport with these day-tour companies.

She keyed the intercom and called a quick vendor meeting. Two of the merchants didn't come up front, but Haley had no time to hunt them down. Not with poor Tyler's tummy problems.

"I've got to leave."

Was it her imagination or did several vendors look relieved?

"Tyler is sick, he's throwing up and I can't leave him with Charlie Simmons like that."

"Of course not." A murmur of agreement riffled through the group of shop owners.

"Lisa, can you stay late again?"

"Sure." She nodded from her place at the back of the group.

"Me, too."

"I'm in," called out another vendor.

"And if it gets too crazy, Viola and Twila said they'd rather be working than sitting home."

"Really?" Haley had tried so hard to be conscientious of the vendors working timeshares that she never thought that some of them might prefer working to not working. "Can you call them if it gets busy?"

"I'll call them before it gets busy," the older man promised, smiling. "It takes them two a little while to find their car and get down the road."

His words lightened the moment and made Haley smile. "The bus schedule is printed on the back wall here and in your dailies," she reminded them as she tugged on her coat. "And tomorrow is our second fire safety inspection. And if we don't pass this time, we could be fined. Or shut down. And—" she hated to reveal this last part, but the seriousness of Brett's inspection pushed her to total honesty "—if we don't pass, the next installment of my bank loan remains in escrow and I can't pay the second round of contractors."

Murmurs of surprise had her raising her hand. "We're not in financial trouble as long as this inspection goes through. The bank's clause says that lack of code adherence is reason to hold our money. So passing this time is crucial."

"We'll pass it." Maude McGinnity's voice came loud and firm from the back. "Having a new business this close to the interstate is good for all of us, Haley. We'll make sure it's done and done right. You've got my word on it."

"And mine."

"Mine, too." Lisa held up the cooperative's copy of the last inspection. "I've got a copy here of what we've fixed since Monday. I'll make everyone their own copy. That way we can double check everything tonight."

"Great idea."

"Perfect!"

"Thank you, everyone." Haley smiled her appreciation as she grabbed her purse, gloves and scarf. "And if anybody knows anything about settling a little boy's stomach, let me know. Business I get." She swept the inviting co-op a quick glance. "Kids? Not so much."

"Ginger ale."

"Time."

"Both," laughed Maude as she waved goodbye. "You'll figure it out, honey. We all do."

Would she?

Haley hoped so. But her lack of knowledge said she should at least order books about child raising. Maybe take a class. Although where she'd fit that into her already-overcrowded schedule, she had no idea. Which meant the idea would go nowhere, but finding a book? Checking with the experts?

That she could do.

"Hey, Charlie. What's up? Are the boys behaving themselves?" Brett reached into the SUV to procure his clipboard as he answered the phone mid-afternoon.

"I don't have 'em," Charlie reported. He sounded glum. "Tyler got sick and I had to call Haley to come get them, what with Jess's baby being small and all."

"Is he all right?" Brett's head leaped to worst-case scenarios. Hospitals. Ambulances.

"Mother says it's just a stomach bug going around," Charlie assured him, "but women are always calmer with this sort of thing than us men."

Not Brett's mother. Joanna Stanton had never been the norm. Maybe most women were calm, cool and collected with sick kids. He wouldn't know. "She's got the boys back at the apartment?"

"Yes. And I was going to take them to see Bwana Jim and the animals." Charlie sounded genuinely disappointed.

"They'd love that, Charlie. Next week maybe?"

"We'll try that," Charlie agreed. "I'm here at the store with Mother. They've had busloads of people 'cross the way, but we don't get much drift from the buses."

But Haley's new business did. And instead of being there, manning the front, steering foot traffic and welcoming folks, she was home with a sick kid. "I'll do this last inspection, then head back there, but I'm on the opposite end of the county, so it will be a while."

"Okay, boss."

Brett keyed Haley's number as a van pulled up alongside his SUV. He slipped the phone back into his pocket, wishing he'd had a chance to talk to her. Assess the situation.

It's a sick kid. Not a coup staged by rebel insurgents. Get a hold of yourself. This stuff happens all the time.

It probably did, Brett realized. But he'd never been a part of it, and having it happen to Haley's little fellows tugged his attention back to Jamison when what he needed to do was concentrate on this inspection.

He shook the owner's hand and tried to separate himself from his concern. That lasted all of five seconds. With a word of apology, he excused himself and hit her number.

"Brett?"

The need in her one-word salutation made him wish he was there helping. Taking care of her and those kids. "I just talked to Charlie. He said Tyler's sick. How's he doing? Do we need to take him in? Have him seen by a doctor?"

"Not according to LuAnn," Haley told him.

Exactly what Charlie had said, so why did he need this confirmation? Because he wanted to hear Haley's voice. Reassure her. Be there for her. "And LuAnn's raised a bunch of kids."

"Exactly," Haley agreed. "She says it just needs to run its course and if he's not better in two days, then we take him in. Or if his fever goes crazy-high, but it's not. Hovering just over a hundred degrees."

"Poor little guy."

"I know." Commiseration colored her tone.

"And you've got the co-op covered?"

"I hope so. Everyone seemed willing to rise to the occasion, but I hate being so close and not know what's going on. How things are developing. We had a bunch of scheduled buses today, and Lisa called to tell me there were two unscheduled ones that stopped."

"And you're torn between duties."

"Yes." She sighed. "But there's no other option, so I'm snuggling my little friend here. LuAnn dropped off a bunch of DVDs, so we're just chillin' together. The three of us."

A slight movement reminded Brett he had a job to do. "I'll stop by the store and grab some sick-kid supplies on my way home. See you later."

"Okay."

He pocketed the phone and turned. The construction crew chief aimed a look of understanding at his pocket. "You've got a sick kid?"

Not exactly, but… "Yes."

The other man swung the door wide. "I hate when they get sick. I don't mind working I beams or scaling scaffolding, but have my kid run a temperature, and I'm running around, wondering what to do to make it better."

His words echoed Brett's feelings. "That's normal, huh?"

The other man laughed and clapped Brett on the back. "A new father, eh? Well, buddy, you're in for the ride of your life."

Was he?

He wanted to be, he realized. In a way that he never wanted anything else, he longed to be special to Haley and those boys, which was downright silly considering the short length of time they'd known each other. But his growing sense of inner peace made him feel almost whole again.

He went through the inspection step by step, resolute, but once done, he went to the Tops Market in Wellsville and stocked up on things Haley might need, then aimed for Jamison, determined to check out Tyler for himself. And maybe give Haley the reassuring hug he needed.

Chapter Eleven

"Don't come near me." Haley issued the edict when she swung open the apartment door.

Brett feigned a fearful expression as he hauled in four plastic sacks filled with everything he thought might be necessary. "Because?"

"I'm probably germ-infested. And I smell bad. The whole apartment smells bad and we might be dealing with plague."

He hugged her anyway, but stayed off topics like last night's kiss. Or his proximity to the boys all day yesterday. Sharing food. Swapping germs. If he was going to catch this bug, most likely it was already working in his system. He released Haley and crossed the room to see Tyler. "Luckily I had my anti-plague shots before my last tour of duty."

"Oh. Well…" She read the humor in his gaze and challenged it. "You're not funny."

"Sure I am. Hey, how're you doin', sport?"

"Brett!" Todd scrambled out of the bathroom, a

toothbrush dripping water as he ran. "Tyler puked all over Charlie's kitchen!"

"Todd."

"Well, he did." Todd stuck a belligerent chin into the air. "I saw him. Gross." He rolled out the last word as he clutched his gut, made gagging noises and pretended to faint onto the floor.

"Poor Charlie. I feel so bad that it happened on his watch."

"Charlie's old-school army." Brett pressed a gentle hand to Tyler's forehead. Not bad, he decided. "And raised three kids. He's tough. Are you guys hungry?"

Todd nodded, emphatic.

Tyler paled. "No, thank you."

"Okay, sport." Brett hauled the five-year-old out of the chair, sat down and cuddled the boy on his lap. The chair was not man-sized, he realized. Short in the leg and not broad-backed like his recliner at home. He turned this way and that, struggling to find a comfortable position. There wasn't one.

"Use the couch."

He turned.

Haley's look of understanding met him full force. She got it, he realized. And him. That he needed to be part of the child's healing. His comfort. "Good idea."

He switched spots, stretched out, and he and Tyler watched a double-length feature of the Magic School Bus's adventures in the human body.

"This is my favorite part," yelled Todd as the cartoon bus descended into the lower intestine.

"I'm not watching," Haley called out. "I've seen it twice already because gastrointestinal issues seem to fascinate little boys."

"The workings of the human body border on miraculous," Brett called back, laughing. "And it's good to know yourself."

"Not that much." She poked her head around the corner. "I've got grilled cheese for you and Todd. You still feeling okay, Todd?"

He rolled on the floor, dramatic to the end. "I'm fine. Stop asking me. Pwease."

"I expect he'll tell us when he doesn't. Or—" Brett's gaze slid back to the descriptive small-intestine screen on the vintage TV "—we'll have evidence to the contrary."

He said "we'll," like his help was a given.

Brett's assumption made her nervous.

It shouldn't, but it did.

His appearance into her life made things feel better. More complete. But she'd counted on folks before. Her father. Her mother. Her stepfather. All had let her down.

He's nothing like any of them.

Haley recognized that, but she didn't dare trust her instincts where men were concerned. In a life riddled by divorce and broken relationships, keeping her guard up simplified matters. But not around Brett, and that was becoming a concern.

Her phone buzzed as she handed Brett and Todd

their sandwiches. She stepped away, noted the out-of-town number and answered, puzzled. "Hello."

Nothing. Again.

She stepped out the apartment door, hoping for a better signal. She'd gotten a call from this number the previous day and had let it go to voice mail, but the caller didn't leave a message. "Hello?"

Still nothing.

Haley disconnected, went back inside and decided to check out the number's location on the internet once the boys were in bed.

"Trouble?" Brett gave the phone a quick glance as she reentered the small living room.

"No one there."

He frowned. "Telemarketers shouldn't have access to our cell phone numbers."

"I won't argue that." She sank to the floor with her sandwich. Todd curled up alongside her, and his presence made her feel like the day hadn't been a total loss.

"If you want to head over to the co-op and check things out, I'll hang here with the boys. I know you've got concerns." He didn't mention tomorrow's fire inspection per se, but she got the drift.

"Several of the vendors promised to go over the list and double-check things. Make sure everything's in order."

"But you're dying to double-check."

She frowned, dismayed. "I am. And that makes me feel guilty, although why I should feel guilty about running a sound business that I've invested time, money and energy in is beyond me."

"The only way to make a man feel trustworthy is to trust him," Brett quoted. "Henry Stimson, secretary of war under multiple presidents. Sound advice."

"Because trust breeds responsibility," Haley noted.

He grinned. "That's my girl."

Such a simple phrase to make her feel so warm inside. Two weeks ago she'd have scoffed at the notion of being someone's girl. Romance and trust hadn't made her short list ever.

Now?

She colored just thinking of it. And Brett's easy smile said he caught the reaction. She had a feeling not much got by a man like Brett Stanton and she wasn't sure if that was good or bad. But right now, with Tyler snuggled along Brett's side, and Todd curled up next to her, her world felt good despite the sick kid and the pending fire inspection. "If I go over there, I look like I don't have faith in them."

"Yes."

She contemplated that, then shrugged. "I'll go first thing in the morning and double-check as long as the boys are doing better. Can you—"

He cut off the request with a nod. "I'll be here at eight. You go over and check things out. That way you can be sure to be ready for my noon inspection."

"Thank you, Brett. You don't have to do all this, you know."

He turned, surprised. "Of course I do. We're friends."

Friends.

She liked being his friend. Having a friend. But she'd thoroughly enjoyed that kiss, and it wasn't exactly a friendly peck on the cheek.

He winked at her.

Heat climbed her cheeks. Internal warning lights flagged her to slow down. Proceed with caution. The boys were vulnerable. Young. They'd already endured more than should be possible in their short lifetimes.

She longed to talk things over with him, but with the boys awake, she didn't dare. No way was she going to risk their losing anyone else, not if she could help it. She knew the merry-go-round of multiple parents and these boys had been through the wringer. No more.

Once the boys were tucked into bed, Brett waved her to the couch. "You sit there. It's more comfortable. Let me tell you what I found out today before I head to the store to close things out."

Guilt prickled her. "I'm sorry, Brett. I know you've got things to do. A business to run."

"I pay Charlie and LuAnn to do that, although I can't say I mind helping out now," he replied. "A lot of interesting folks travel the interstates these days. So." He drew out a small notebook and tore out a page. "This is Dr. Jackson's number. I set up an appointment for the boys for next Tuesday. They're scheduled to see Katie Bascomb, the nurse practitioner. The court clerk called me back today and put us on the Surrogate Court schedule for Monday morning."

"And if they give me guardianship…"

"Then we can either reimmunize the boys or do the blood tests. Either way, Tyler should be able to get in a couple of weeks of school before the Christmas break."

"Christmas." She sent him a look of panic. "I have to figure out Christmas with the boys. I don't even have a candle burning in the window. No wreath. No tree."

"Christmas isn't all about decorations or gifts."

"I know." She met his gaze. "But even if I don't go over-the-top, it requires thought and timing. And I seem to be losing my grip on both these days."

"We have weeks yet."

"Weeks of hopefully record sales next door," she reminded him. "Although with Tyler in school and Todd in day care—"

Brett cleared his throat. "About that."

"About?" She paused, puzzled. "What?"

"Todd doesn't need to go to day care."

"Sure he does," she answered quickly. "I can't watch him at the co-op, Brett."

"I'll watch him."

Red flags sprang up throughout her brain. "No, you can't do that. It's too much."

"It's not," he countered. "I'm free. My business is being managed by two very capable people, my time is my own when I'm not helping cover for Bud Schmidt and if I get a fire call, I'll have LuAnn or Charlie step in."

"Brett, I can't let you do that."

"Why not?"

Because I don't trust men to keep their word? Because I can't risk Todd's feelings and involvement with you and have you wave goodbye to him a few months down the line? Because while I can handle business risk, I shy away from personal involvement?

She'd sound like an emotional train wreck if she laid all that at his door. And she wasn't. Being careful did not equal being neurotic.

Although right now, facing his confused expression while she hesitated, she felt neurotic. And protective. And out of her league.

He stood.

So did she.

"We'll talk about this next week." He moved to the door, and Haley had no trouble seeing the military carriage of the man before her. Back straight, shoulders tight, chin up.

She'd just dissed a soldier which made her feel like a first-class jerk, but she needed time to assess things and every time she thought she gained a handle on her new responsibilities, something jerked the rug out from under her.

"I'll be here at eight, okay?"

She nodded, wishing she'd had time to consider his offer, longing to take back her quick rejection. "Yes. Thank you."

Her words sounded hollow. She'd taken a step back when what she longed to do was move forward. Hesitation didn't become her. And tonight, as he walked out the door, she felt like he was walking away.

But that was silly, right? Because he'd be back tomorrow morning. He'd said so.

He trudged across the angled parking lot, cutting a bee-line path to his store across the two-lane road. Rain poured down on him, steady. Relentless. He didn't run. He didn't reach up a hand to cover his head. He did nothing to stop the onslaught, his upright stance brave and true.

And that just made her feel smaller inside.

Chapter Twelve

"I'm giving you a green light." Brett's flat expression dulled the happy moment as he and Haley rounded the last corner of Bennington Station's second floor the next afternoon. He tapped his clipboard lightly. "Full approval. You're good to go." He signed off and gave Haley a copy for her records and one for the bank. "This should clear the draft they've been holding."

She should be dancing in the streets, knowing the money would finally be available. Her debts would be satisfied and she'd have a personal savings account again. Small, but small was a big step up from nothing. "Thank you, Brett."

She started to reach for his arm, but he turned, leaving her hand fluttering. Had he done that deliberately?

Well, why not after she'd shrugged him off last night?

"I'll file my copies right away," he told her as he moved toward the exit. He'd kept his jacket on, as if planning a quick escape. Her fault, she knew. "That way if the bank double-checks through the computer, you're good to go."

"Thank you. Again."

"Just doing my job." No little smile. No easy, long, lingering look. "Once I've got that squared away, I'll take over with the boys and let Charlie go home. If you don't mind."

"Of course I don't mind. I just—"

He held up a hand. "I get it, Haley. It's not a problem."

It *was* a problem and he didn't get it because she was having trouble understanding her mix of feelings herself. Why had she let her buttons get pushed like that? Why did she build walls when it came to a man like Brett?

A man like Brett? How much do you know about him? Almost nothing. You've done what you should do to protect those boys. They're your primary responsibility now.

Except she was never there. Brett was. Which only made things more confusing. "I'll see you later."

He nodded and left, not angry, but...resigned. Once again she sensed the military person within. Strong. Unintimidated. Resourceful.

"Oh, mama, that is one gorgeous guy."

Lisa's vocal approval underlined what Haley already knew. "He's very nice."

"Well, there's that." Lisa nodded, slipped a piece of chocolate to the college girl working the front checkout and then offered one to Haley with a wink. "And to-die-for good-looking, in case you hadn't noticed."

How could she not notice? Rather than admit it, she changed the subject. "Well, he's been a huge help with the boys. I felt bad having him watch them today in case either one gets sick to their stomach, but he assured me he's done latrine duty before."

Lisa laughed. "He said that?"

"Yes. Why?"

"Because I don't think colonels see a lot of bathroom duty in the service."

"Colonel?"

"Colonel Brett Stanton, U.S. Army, retired." Lisa turned, puzzled. "You really didn't know?"

Haley shook her head. Lisa's revelation made her concerns seem sillier. No one got to the rank of colonel if they reneged on their duty, right?

"It's nice to see him out and about." Lisa accepted the day's mail from the mailman, handed it off to Haley and started walking away.

"Why wasn't he out and about before?"

Lisa turned. Her expression blended surprise and hesitation. Then she sighed, remembering. "I forgot, you weren't here back then and you've been crazy-busy since you arrived last spring." She exchanged a reluctant look with the desk clerk and shrugged acceptance. "It's not a secret. I just thought he might have mentioned it to you."

Haley lifted an eyebrow and waited, silent.

"His son, Josiah."

"And this son is?" Haley left the question open-ended for Lisa to fill in the blank. She did.

"He's dead, Haley."

That was not what Haley expected. Lisa's expression said there was more to tell. "How?"

"Afghanistan. Two years ago. About the same time your brother, Anthony, was killed."

The surge.

"Oh, Lisa." Haley closed the distance between them and kept her voice low. "His son was in the service?"

"He had him young. Very young. But Brett was career army and he and Deb never got married. He supported Joe, but didn't get to see him often."

"And now he's gone." Haley understood absentee fathers. Too well. Her biological father had left three kids high and dry, and her stepfather was more interested in status than the child that came with marrying her mother. But poor Brett...

Lisa's lips thinned. "Brett took it hard. He had just retired when it happened."

"I don't know what to say."

"I'm sorry." Lisa's voice reflected her discomfort. "I wouldn't have told you if it was private, but the whole town knows. There was a huge parade, bringing Joe home. People lined the streets, waving flags. Crying. Praying. You couldn't get near the cemetery because of how many veterans turned out to lay him to rest. Except..."

Haley frowned, waiting.

"Brett didn't attend the services."

"He missed his own son's funeral?" Haley tried to imagine why anyone would do that. She couldn't.

"He stayed home. And he's kind of stayed home ever since," Lisa continued. "Other than his involvement with the fire department, he stayed under the radar. Totally. Until Thanksgiving, that is."

Until he met me.

The insinuation seemed crazy, but deep within, Haley recognized the truth. Something had clicked that day, for both of them. Something warm and nice and blessed. A connection unlike any other.

Really? That's what you're going with? Doesn't every smitten girl think the same thing?

Haley hushed the internal voice. Maybe the warning held merit. Maybe not. In any case, how would she know if she never gave anyone the chance? And by anyone, she meant Brett.

"Hey, I—"

"Don't apologize," Haley assured Lisa. "I'm glad you told me. It explains a lot, like why I never met him over the summer. And people's reactions when he walks into a room."

"People have been concerned." Lisa didn't need to say more. "They're glad to see him doing better."

Until she'd shut him down the night before. What must he think of her? Probably no more than she thought of herself right now. She had no idea how to fix this, and as a bus pulled into the loop adjacent to Bennington Station's decorative entry, she knew she had to re-direct her thoughts to work. But tonight?

Tonight she and Brett would have a talk.

* * *

The emergency call came in as Brett took a pot of chicken noodle soup off the stove. Charlie hurried in through the back door. "I heard the monitor. Accident on I-86, just east of Karr Valley Road. Cars overturned. One's on fire. You go. I've got the boys."

Brett kissed the tops of both boys' heads, grabbed his keys and moved to the door. "Thanks, Charlie. Haley should be here in a couple of hours."

"Don't matter. I've got all night."

"Where are you going?" Todd raced across the room and encircled Brett's leg in an iron grip. "I don't want you to go. Pwease?"

Oh, man.

Brett bent and met the little guy's gaze. "I have to, Todd. I'm a fireman, remember? Someone's in trouble and they need me. Right now."

"Todd, he told us that," Tyler scolded. "Sometimes he has to help people. Let go!"

Tyler's imperious older-brother voice didn't help matters. Todd clung tighter. "Can I come, too? I want to be with you!"

Brett's heart ground to a halt. A link of that rusty chain grabbed hold again, remembering how little time he'd spent with Josiah. "Sorry, bud. I've got to go. Charlie will stay with you until Aunt Haley gets here. And I'll explain tomorrow, okay?"

Charlie disengaged the little boy from Brett's leg. Todd set up a wail.

Tyler scowled.

Derringer leaped to his feet, tail wagging, following Brett to the door. Riding shotgun to emergencies was Derringer's job, and the hound took it seriously.

"Derringer, don't go! Don't go! Don't weave me! Pwease!"

Brett patted the dog's head, gazed into his cinnamon-toned eyes and gave the command. "Stay."

The dog frowned, perplexed. But then he shifted his head as if assessing the moment. Dropping his chin, he turned and went to stand alongside Charlie and Todd. He nudged Todd's leg with his muzzle as if to reassure the boy, then set a big, red paw on Charlie's thigh. He let out a doggie sigh that said he understood his new command, even if he didn't like it.

Brett hurried out, torn.

Had Josiah missed him like this each time he deployed? Was this what Deb went through every time something changed in the boy's life? Was Todd's reaction normal or just an overwrought, tired little boy who got nervous with change?

Brett suspected a combination. Todd's life had been riddled with unexpected turns. He and Tyler didn't have a norm. And what Brett had hoped to be the norm now seemed at odds with their guardian's wishes.

So be it.

He couldn't risk setting them up for disappointment. He'd mistaken Haley's gratitude for something more. His fault. But he was man enough to know how to respect a line drawn in the sand. He'd still help, but he'd keep his distance. Better all around that way.

It didn't feel better, but once he rolled up to the accident scene, he shoved everything else out of mind. Wandering thoughts had no place there.

Jaws of Life.

Gas-fed fire.

Cold rain.

Life-threatening injuries.

The senseless, brutal accident numbed Brett's brain. By ten o'clock that night he was wet, tired and discouraged. *God, watch over them. Heal them. Help them. Please.*

A drunk driver and a teen going too fast for the wet road conditions. Both now grappled for their lives after being airlifted to the University of Rochester Medical Center via Mercy Flight. The first responders had closed the interstate to allow the choppers room to set down. That had been dicey in the wet conditions, but at least the predicted snow had held off. This deep in the hills, ninety minutes by ground from the nearest trauma center, critical care victims might spend that first crucial hour in the back of an ambulance on slick roads if the helicopters were grounded by inclement weather.

Derringer rushed to meet Brett as he came through the door, eager to make sure his owner was all right. Brett bent low, rubbed the dog's head between the ears and met the coonhound's eyes. "Thanks for staying, old man. Better that you be here, taking care of the boys. You're okay with that, right?"

The dog's look said maybe he was and maybe he wasn't, but when Brett read Charlie's note, the old man's perception made him realize he'd made the right decision.

Todd settled down right after you left. Tyler and I played War with your cards. Todd and Derringer played with the big trains and watched *Thomas the Tank Engine*. Both fell asleep. Luckily Haley came by before I joined them. Whatever happened to action cartoons like Road Runner? And that crazy coyote that was always chasing after him? My kids loved them things. I told Haley that Mother and I would watch the boys early tomorrow in case you need to sleep in.

What would he do without Charlie and LuAnn? What had he done to deserve such good friends?

He settled into the recliner and picked up his Bible. He knew right where to go. Where he always went when the day's events pulled him down. The thirty-ninth Psalm, a prayer of need and grace… "Withhold not thou, O Lord, thy tender mercies from me; thy mercy and thy truth have always upheld me. For evils without number have surrounded me; my iniquities have overtaken me, and I was not able to see."

He'd done his best tonight, and it still might not

be enough. Both drivers might perish, their fate in God's hands.

Why didn't someone stop the drunkard from getting behind the wheel? Why didn't the kid's parents tell him to slow down and take it easy?

Why didn't you advise Josiah against the military? Why didn't you fill your son with stories of war? Death? Destruction?

He dropped his head into his hands, running the reasoning full circle. This country was worth fighting for. He believed that. But he hated that it cost him his son. His brother. His mother's lapse of sobriety. And Deb's loss of her child.

At what cost, freedom?

He knew the answer. Any cost.

But he longed for a world through the prophet Isaiah's eyes, where the lion lay down with the lamb and peace reigned.

He lay back, hands clasped over the book, and closed his eyes. Sleep came briefly before another alarm roused him. This time a fire, a house fire, not far from where the old fire tower used to stand. Rushing, he tugged on his gear with automatic precision, a soldier trait that worked well for firemen, too.

The rain had turned to a wet, slushy snow, enough to muck the roads. The plows hadn't been commissioned yet. Brett radioed the fire crew that he was en route and advised them of road conditions. He turned east, knowing the first trucks to respond would be close behind him.

And even knowing that, as his SUV took the Jersey Hill fork off of County Road 2A, the orange glow melded to peach spires with the falling snow. Eerily beautiful, the sight clenched his gut. Had everyone gotten out? Were they safe?

Derringer made a commiserative noise in the back of his throat, his worried sound echoing Brett's concern. Brett screeched to a halt, barreled out of the driver's side and came around.

"Help him! Oh, please, please, help him!"

A nightgown-clad woman's cries pierced the night. The roar of the fully involved fire dulled Brett's hearing. He saw a man dressed in nothing but pajama pants trying to find a way into the burning home.

Which meant someone hadn't made it out yet. "Who's in there? In the house?"

She clapped a hand over her face, unable to speak.

Brett grasped her upper arms in a firm brace. "Help me. Which room?"

"The second one on the second floor. On that side." She waved her hand to the right. "My son, Nick. Oh, my son..."

Brett raced for the house. "Stay back!" He pulled the man away.

Sirens screamed closer, but with no one else on-site yet, Brett had to restrain the man from trying to fight the flames and rescue the child. Because it couldn't be too late. He refused to consider that possibility.

Firm hands grabbed the crying man from behind. "Go. I've got him." Two firefighters joined up alongside Brett. A host of others now milled the perimeter, setting up hoses, the sound of male voices pricked with the woman's cries.

There was no way in the front door. Left open, the brisk wind fanned the flames from front to back, feeding the fire an oxygen-heavy diet. If only they'd thought to close the door.

They hadn't, and the front was fully engulfed.

Firefighters raced around the front corner, aiming for the northern exposure. The fire wasn't as bold here. Maybe… Just maybe…

Overgrown bushes burned beneath the boy's east-side bedroom window. Flames licked the underside of the frame. There'd be no entrance there. They moved to the next available window, around the back corner of the house.

Much better. The house blocked the wind and the second-story window was accessible from the ladder.

A group of men hoisted the ladder into place and braced themselves. Brett and two other firemen scrambled up. Using his metal bar, Brett broke the second-story window. Smoke billowed forth. Darkness swallowed him as he crawled through the opening, peering through his mask and the thick, pungent smoke. Smithy followed him in, while another fireman manned a hose to provide cover water.

The mother had indicated a room that now lay to Brett's left. He bent low, fighting his way forward. Smithy edged up alongside him. He motioned left. Brett agreed. They moved in tandem, the roar of flames pushed their way by the west wind. The jet of back water might help, but it couldn't buy them much time, and time was of the essence. A wind-fed fire. Snow instead of rain. A trapped child.

Brett prayed the boy hadn't tried to go downstairs. He wanted to locate the room and find a living, breathing, scared child behind a closed door that kept the bulk of the smoke at bay.

Feeling along the wall, they found a door. It refused to open, as if weighted by some strong, low force. No kid could put that much pressure against a standard bedroom door, but it took Brett and Smithy long seconds to push the door open enough to get through. Just as Brett pulled out his hatchet to chop their way in, the door gave way to their combined muscle.

Smithy went first.

He tripped instantly, and the way he went down told Brett that he didn't trip over a kid's toy or a rolled-up sheet.

Smithy fell over a body.

Brett's heart seized. He hauled Smithy up and fought the bile rising in his throat. He reached down to retrieve the boy's body, praying he might not be gone, begging the angels and saints to bring any help they could muster.

Smithy grabbed Brett's arm. Pointed his light.

A dog.

Smithy had tripped over a dog.

Brett panned his light around the room.

Nothing.

But the kid wouldn't have shut the dog in the room. Brett knew that. Kids reacted instinctively.

He'd hide from the fire.

Smithy aimed his flashlight beneath the bed.

Nothing.

Brett wrenched open the closet door, half afraid of what he'd find on the other side.

A boy, older than Tyler. Scared. Crying. Silent wails contorted the boy's face, his voice no match against the fire's roar.

But alive.

Brett reached in and hauled the boy up. "I've got you, fellow. I've got you."

Smithy cleared the way for them to work themselves back to the window.

Flames pulsed up the stairway to their left. A crackling roar overhead said the roof was involved. That meant it could come crashing in at any moment.

Smithy led the way, buddying with Brett, making sure no obstacles blocked their path. They made it into the other bedroom and over to the window.

The other firefighter stood there, arms out, waiting for the boy. Even backlit from the high-intensity lights now aimed at the house, Brett saw the relief on his face when the boy jerked, showing he was alive.

He took the boy.

Brett climbed out and followed, but not before turning back to Smithy. The older man grasped his arm and shook his head.

Brett knew that look.

The dog was gone.

And he knew he shouldn't have even considered going back in for the animal, but knowing that Derringer sat in the SUV, watching and waiting for his master's return, made Brett want a full happy ending.

But as much as he loved Derringer, he understood one thing: Dogs weren't people. Their job now was to save what they could and pray for that boy and his parents.

The medics had the boy on oxygen and strapped to a gurney by the time Brett and Smithy made it down. The boy's mother was wrapped in a blanket and someone's coat. The father had been given a sweatshirt. As Brett advanced, a neighbor came running up the driveway with warm clothes for the parents.

"Nick! Oh, Nick!" The mother threw her arms around the boy. Tears streamed down her face, joy mixed with hysteria. "Oh, baby, I was so scared! Let me look at you...."

The medic stepped back. "Quickly, ma'am. We need to keep him on oxygen."

Nick's cough underscored the medic's concern, but the boy reached up a hand to his mother. "Where's Bailey?"

The mother straightened. Chagrin and sorrow deepened lines in her face. "Oh, Nick, I—"

"Is that your dog, son?" Brett asked.

The boy nodded as they loaded him into the back of the rescue wagon ambulance. "Yeah. She wouldn't let me out. I kept trying, but she laid down in front of the door and growled at me."

The mother shook her head. "Bailey would never growl at you, Nick. She loved you."

Oh, she'd loved him, Brett realized. Enough to lay down her life for him. He stepped alongside the mother and put a hand out to the boy. "She saved you, son."

Nick frowned, not understanding.

Brett thrust his chin back toward the burning house. "She laid down against the door so you wouldn't go through it. The hall was on fire. The stairs were already collapsing. There's no way you would have made it out."

Brett shifted slightly and met the mother's gaze. "The dog blocked the door so Nick couldn't get out and smoke couldn't get in. But she was gone by the time we got into the room."

"She's…" The boy's face crumpled as realization set in.

Brett nodded. "I'm sorry, son. But I can tell you one thing, that dog loved you till the end."

The man gripped his wife.

Tears streamed down the little boy's cheeks. His mother and father were no better.

The medic intervened. "He needs this." He held up the oxygen mask and settled Nick back into a reclining position. "You folks hop in. Let's roll."

"But—"

The man turned as if wishing he could do something. A second medic climbed into the back. "Sir, leave it to the experts. They've got the gear. Let's get your boy looked at, okay?"

The father nodded agreement. The mother bent low, checking her child, her face sad but no longer tormented.

They'd lost their home, but homes could be rebuilt. They'd lost their dog, but as sad as that was, Piney Hitchcock kept plenty more down at the pound in Wellsville. The main thing was that they'd kept their child and that was reason enough to thank God right there.

Chapter Thirteen

Brett was avoiding her.

Haley drew that conclusion when Charlie showed up the next morning to get the boys. Sure, he said Brett had a fire call, but Haley knew they'd left things at an uncomfortable impasse two days before. To her, Brett's avoidance made perfect sense, but one way or another, she'd talk to him. Hash this out.

"Do you have to work again today?" Tyler whined the question into more syllables than could ever be considered necessary.

"I do." She rumpled his hair. "But once Christmas is over, life will settle down."

"I don't even fink Cwistmas is coming," objected Todd. He looked around their austere apartment as Charlie handed him his jacket. "It doesn't wook wike Cwistmas here."

Nailed by a three-year-old. Haley sighed and made a face of commiseration. "I know. I'm sorry I've been so busy. Maybe this weekend we can do some decorating."

"Really?"

"You mean it?"

Uh-oh. They were looking for promises. Promises she wasn't sure she could keep and therefore should not make. "I said maybe. That means I'm not sure how work will be going, so we've got to balance things out."

Tyler scowled. "I don't think we're very balanced."

Haley knew what he meant, but had little recourse. "We'll get more balanced after the holidays. That I will promise."

Charlie herded the boys out the door. "They'll be fine. Mother's making Christmas cookies with them this morning."

Todd's face lit up. Tyler's grin made Haley feel two feet tall. Such a little thing, to make cookies with the boys. If only…

Charlie waved and winked. "They'll be fine. Stop beating yourself up. Haven't you heard it takes a village to raise a child?"

But it shouldn't, Haley realized. Not under ideal circumstances. It should take a set of parents, equally invested.

Because that hadn't been the norm in her world, she wasn't certain such a thing still existed except in commercials, where a whole happy family gathered around the amazing scent of freshly brewed coffee on Christmas morning.

It's a commercial, made to sell a product. Do a reality check, Haley. You've got a growing business, the boys are settling in, and you've got your whole life ahead of you. What more could you possibly want? You're living your dream.

The answer hit as she rounded the corner of the former furniture showroom and saw Brett's house tucked behind a copse of trees.

She missed him, which was silly because she saw him yesterday, right? But she missed the easy warmth, his steady look, the gentle strength that surrounded him.

And now, knowing about his son...

She turned into the co-op, wishing she had guts enough to march across the street and wake him up. Make him listen to her. Apologize for being nervous and drawing back.

And make a fool of yourself? Really? Is that what you're after? Because that's what's going to happen. Plan your work. Work your plan. That strategy has worked so far. Why change things?

"Haley, good morning!" Maude McGinnity walked toward her from the employee parking area.

"Maude." She hurried to the older woman's side and offered her arm to help the elderly woman through the slush. "Don't park over there. Park closer."

"And admit I'm old?" Maude drew back, feigning surprise. "Not on your life, child. But I do appreciate your help. This slush is rough on old feet."

"The boys are hoping we get real snow soon," Haley added as they made their way in. "The forecast says more rain, so this will be gone by nightfall most likely." She slowed her step to match Maude's and felt good doing it. Almost like she could calm down and take a breath with the older woman. "And we got the boys outdoor gear last week, so they can play when it does happen."

"These are the days to remember," Maude told her. "And they fly by, Haley. Don't let this—" she aimed her gaze toward Bennington Station's front door "—overshadow that. Make time for both."

Haley saw the wisdom in the words, but it wasn't as easy as it sounded. "This is a tough time of year to be taking time off from a new business, Maude. There's so much to do. I second-guess myself. I wonder if we should have waited and not pushed to open for this Christmas season."

"Financially, this was the smartest move," Maude replied. "But then you got those precious boys and it's a wonder how to handle both."

"It is."

"Let folks help more." Maude walked through the door that Haley swung wide, and turned back once inside. "Be willing to accept help here." She swept the gracious, country entryway a thoughtful look. "And with those boys. You've got people lined up around you, wanting to do more. All's you've got to do is knock down a few of those walls you've built and let them, honey."

Haley met Maude's gaze. "That obvious, huh?"

Maude smiled, patted Haley's arm and turned toward her mini-shop on the first level. "Blatantly, but because you remind me a lot of myself at the same age, I'm going to just keep praying and know you'll find a way to handle things. My suggestion?"

Haley waited, knowing she didn't really have a choice, but that was okay because Maude McGinnity was one of the nicest people on Earth. "Trust the people around you. If one fails you here or there, you've got plenty more to pick up the pieces."

Trust.

There was that issue again, the same one Brett raised the other night. The night she drew back and hurt his feelings.

"I'll try harder." She reached out and hugged the older woman. "Promise."

"Good."

Maude's smile of confidence gave Haley an emotional boost. In fact... "Maude?"

"Yes?" Maude turned back, an eyebrow raised in question.

"I'm going to run a quick errand. I'll be back in a few minutes, okay?"

"Plenty of us will be here to run things if it takes longer than that, honey. You do what you have to do."

"I will." Haley walked back out the door, diagonally crossed the parking lot and the street, then made her way to Brett's door. She paused on the step, uncertain, wondering if she should just do a quiet about-face and head right back to the co-op where she belonged.

"Let me know when you've decided and I'll get you coffee."

She turned, flustered.

Brett stood framed in the back door of the convenience store, a red plaid flannel and blue jeans making him look country rustic and altogether good but tired. Oh, so tired. "I thought you were sleeping."

He considered that statement, then aimed his gaze at the house. "So you wanted to wake me?"

"No."

His frown made fun of her. Just a little. "You *didn't* want to wake me."

"No, I—" She paused and hauled in a breath. Why did this seem so easy when Maude was urging her on? Face-to-face with Brett? Suddenly not so simple. "I wanted to talk to you."

"Ah." He moved forward. Up close, she saw the weariness shadow his eyes. She longed to smooth the angst away, ease the tightness she sensed in him, but she had no right to do either.

He opened the door.

The scent of old smoke hit her in the face.

He turned before she could hide her reaction. "Sorry." He grabbed a pile of things, carried them out to the back porch and tossed them there, then closed the door. "I was called out last night and didn't throw that stuff in the washer. I know it smells bad."

"You weren't expecting company."

"True." He held out his coffee cup. "I meant what I said. I'll be glad to get you coffee. Ramir just made fresh carafes of house blend and hazelnut."

Haley tried to downscale how good the latter

sounded. His hinted smile said she failed, but also gave her a whisper of hope. "Hazelnut. Please."

"I'll be right back."

She walked around the train room while he was gone. Derringer opened one eye, saw who it was and promptly went back to sleep. Dog and master were both physically drained.

She turned as Brett came back into the house through the back door. "Two creams, two sugars and an extra flavor shot."

"My hero."

He winced.

Haley inhaled, set the coffee down, grabbed his hand and led him over to the recliner. "Sit."

"Because?"

"I've got something to say and you make me nervous when you pace like a caged bear. Sit."

"You're bossy today."

It was Haley's turn to make a face. "Every day, actually. According to Maude. And that's why I want to talk to you, Brett."

"Because Maude thinks you're bossy?"

"Because I *am* bossy," she admitted. "And I don't like to accept help. And I try to do everything on my own."

"True on all counts. Why is that, Haley?"

He stayed in his seat, watching her, his face showing little emotion. His nonreaction made the conversation more difficult and she felt a surge of sympathy for miscreant soldiers who ever had to do a face-to-face with their colonel. "I've always had to do things on my own. The whys aren't important now, but I want you to know how much I appreciate your help. And that when I get cautious and bossy, I'd really like for you not to get all stiff-necked and standoffish. Because I don't know how to handle that."

"An impasse, then."

"Are we?" Haley wanted him to say no, to stand up and tell her that he understood her cautious nature and her fears and could overlook them.

He did none of those things. "I enjoy helping with the boys. They enjoy being with me. We can keep it that simple."

Suddenly she didn't want simple at all. Seeing him there, a steady, solid leader whose face showed a night of wear and tear, she realized how immature she must seem to a man of accomplishment and experience. For the life of her, she couldn't imagine why he might have been interested in her in the first place. "So. Simple."

"Yes."

"Okay." She turned to move toward the door, the silence weighing heavy.

"Haley."

"Yes?" She turned, wishing her voice didn't sound so hopeful and expectant, as if waiting for him to drop a crumb in her direction.

"Your coffee."

"Oh." She walked back, picked up the to-go cup and held it up. "Thank you again."

"My pleasure."

He didn't look a bit pleased, but then neither was she. The more she thought about it on the way back to Bennington Station, the more agitated she became. She'd walked over there, humbled herself, kind of asked forgiveness in an offhand way and got a cool rebuff for her troubles.

Her phone rang. She pulled it out of her pocket, hoping it was Brett.

The same out-of-area-code number flashed in the display. Haley scowled, pushed ignore and put the phone away. She meant to check out the number the other night, but she'd forgotten. Later, she promised herself. She went to work, determined to put on a Christmas face for today's customers, the bread and butter of a new enterprise. Walking into the co-op, the prettiness of the hallway struck her a low blow.

Her business was fully decked out for the holidays.

Her apartment was bare.

The shoppers and vendors got full advantage of her love of Christmas.

The boys came home to empty walls and no tree. And she'd used her Nativity set in the co-op, so they didn't even have a manger scene to remind them of the holiness of the upcoming day. Jesus's birthday.

Soon, she promised herself. One way or another she'd make time to decorate. Pretty things up. Help the boys enjoy the anticipation of Christ's birth. She wasn't sure when they'd get to it, but she made a mental promise to prioritize it.

* * *

He was a jerk.

Brett realized that when he woke up around three hours later.

Haley had come over. She'd tried to make amends. And he'd rebuffed her because he was tired and ornery and had just found out that both accident victims died overnight. Despite their best efforts and quick response, both drivers lost their lives.

He shouldn't have talked to her. He should have ducked back into the store when he saw her knocking, but he'd ignored the internal warning so he could see her.

And he'd blown it, big-time.

The Bible lay open from where he'd left it the night before. A passage from Psalm 18, perfect for a soldier's heart and soul. "The Lord is my rock, my fortress and my deliverer; my God is my rock, in whom I take refuge, my shield. I called to the Lord, who is worthy of praise, and I have been saved from my enemies. He rescued me from my powerful enemy, from my foes, who were too strong for me."

Had he? Brett wondered. Had God delivered him through multiple deployments and assignments, from years of doing good, to shy away from a challenge now?

No.

Haley was running scared. From what, he didn't know, but he recognized the symptoms because they mirrored his own. He needed to show her his strength.

Convince her of his investment. Let her see the man of honor inside the wounded soul.

Which meant he needed to toughen up and get back in the game.

Hesitation didn't suit him. As a young soldier, that had caused an occasional problem. Now?

He cleaned up, threw his smoke-filled clothes into the washer, called Charlie and set a plan in motion. Regardless of how she'd end up feeling about him, she needed his help. And the boys needed his time and efforts. Being with them made him feel just plain good about so many things.

He remembered the little boy from the night before. Of how close his parents came to losing their son. The dog, faithful to the end. The accident victims gone, leaving grieving families behind.

"No one knows the day or the hour," proclaimed Matthew in his Gospel. But reasonable people should understand the inevitable, pushing them to live each day to the full. Starting now, Brett was determined to do just that.

Haley's phone buzzed just after a nonexistent lunch. The number display made her hopes rise, but she knew better, didn't she? "Brett?"

"Haley."

His deep voice made her remember that kiss. The way Brett whispered her name.

Earth to Haley. Simple, right? At his request.

She almost forgot, but she heeded the warning for

two very good reasons. Well, three. Todd, Tyler and herself. "What's up?"

"Todd just came down with the stomach bug."

Oh, no.

"He's fine here," Brett went on. "You don't have to leave work, but I knew you'd want to know."

"Brett, thank you, but Charlie and LuAnn can't be watching sick kids."

"I've got them at my place. We were, um…" He paused as if searching for words, then continued, "The boys and I were planning a covert deployment but our battle plan was thwarted by legions of intestinal bacteria."

"Ugh."

"I can't disagree." But he laughed when he said it, as if it wasn't the end of the world. "Anyway, he's resting here at my place, I washed the smoky-smelling stuff so the house smells better, and he's watching Road Runner cartoons on DVDs because Charlie thought the boys' humor education was sadly lacking."

"I love Road Runner," Haley told him. "I love old cartoons. The new ones are just not funny. With the exception of *Phineas and Ferb.* Tyler found it for me, and it's hysterical."

"We'll have to watch it sometime," Brett promised. "Oops. Gotta go. Round two. See you tonight."

He didn't wait for her to reply. Correction: He couldn't wait for her to reply and she frowned in commiseration, imagining the sick little boy and the big guy.

He sounded better. Rested. More like the man she'd first met.

By the time she locked the co-op's door after an amazing day of sales, she was pumped to go home and see Brett. Talk to him. Hug little Todd and be reassured that he was fine.

Charlie greeted her at the door. He read her expression and shrugged. "Brett had a firehouse fund-raiser meeting for the Christkindl Celebration next week. He does the food for the fire department's chicken and biscuits booth."

Right now, chicken and biscuits sounded like haute cuisine. Her gut rumbled in reply to the images in her brain. Soft, puffed biscuits with crispy, golden tops, soaking up puddles of gravy. Tender pieces of white meat, flavored just so.

She fought back a sigh. "How's Todd doing?"

"Much better. He's sleeping. Tyler, too. They got tuckered out between the morning baking marathon and an afternoon of cartoons and the dog."

"They love that dog." Haley tiptoed across the room and peeked into the bedroom. Both boys lay sleeping, covers kicked off, bed tousled. The sight made her smile. In repose they were positively serene.

Awake?

Adorable, but not serene. She backed away from the door and refaced Charlie as he said, "Mother and I love that dog, too. It near broke our hearts, the idea of giving him up, but then Brett came back to town and we realized God put us at a crossroads."

"Literally and figuratively." Haley nodded in the direction of the Crossroads Mini-Mart. "And then He put me on the scene."

"And them boys." Charlie moved forward, gave her a quick hug and stepped back. "'To everything there is a season....'"

"A favorite verse of mine," Haley admitted. "But how do you know when it's God's plan and when it's just pure old temptation?"

"You pray," Charlie said simply.

She'd been remiss in that. So busy depending on herself, she forgot to lay her trust in God. Charlie made blind faith sound easy.

It was anything but.

"When is the Christkindl Market?" she asked.

"Next weekend at the VanAlmeter place across from the park. There's things for kids to do, old-fashioned games, and people take sleigh rides through the park. Once it gets dark, folks drive through the west end of the park for the Festival of Lights. It'll probably put a bite in your business," he noted as he turned for the door. "But only on Saturday."

"The co-op can actually benefit if the market brings folks to town," she assured him. "They've got to drive right by us to get on the interstate, and I'll bet half the folks stop for a look, because the co-op's that pretty."

Charlie grinned. "It's a sight for sore eyes to see that old place up and runnin' again. Your grandpa and great-grandpa sure loved the work they did in that factory back in the day. They were good men, Haley."

She hadn't known Great-grandpa, but Grandpa Bennington had been a "port in a storm" kind of guy, and she'd loved him. That made his bequest all that much more important. She'd waited over a decade to be in a position to do something with the old factory and showroom, but she had no regrets. Except the current time crunch.

"'Night, Haley."

"Good night, Charlie."

He ambled down the steps, his gait unsteady. The slush had frozen into chunked ice and she watched, concerned he might fall. He made it to his car safely, waved and turned the small vehicle toward Jamison.

She'd hoped to see Brett. That hadn't worked out. But the thought of his working on a major fund-raiser to supply Christmas baskets for the needy and toys for children…

The guy had no clue how special he was. Did she? She hoped so.

A knock on the door woke her ninety minutes later. Confused, she sat up.

The knock came again, probing. Insistent. But light, as if not wanting to wake the boys.

She frowned at the door, wishing she'd had the contractors install a security viewing hole. But she'd cut corners on the apartment to allow more funds for Bennington Station. Right now, with someone on the other side of that door in the dead of night, she'd have gladly paid the extra fifty-nine dollars.

"Haley, are you awake?"

Brett.

Relief washed over her. She hurried to the door and gently turned the lock.

He still looked tired, but then so was she and she hadn't fought a fire in the predawn hours. "Are you feeling better?"

"Yes, thanks." He strode in with purpose, carrying a toolbox, his gaze moving left and right. Then up and down. He crossed the living room floor and quietly opened the door to the bedroom. Removing a penlight-sized flashlight from his pocket, he scanned the bedroom ceiling, nodded and closed the door. "Good." He turned to face her.

"What's good?"

"Smoke detectors. One in the kitchen, one in the bedroom. Now we just need one here." He pointed up to the ceiling, then pulled a new smoke detector unit from the toolbox. "This will take only a few minutes."

"You're doing that now?" Her voice squeaked, imagining the boys waking up, tumbling out of bed, excited to see Brett. She and the boys had a lot in common, but she bit back the sigh that thought inspired. "It's almost eleven. You really think this is a good idea?"

"Yes."

He withdrew a small battery-operated drill and retrieved a kitchen chair to give him enough lift to reach the ceiling.

"You'll fall."

"Not if you hold the chair."

Did he mean it? She held the chair in any case, certain that if he tumbled she'd be dealing with two little kids all night long. "This couldn't wait?"

He shook his head, marked two holes for the mount, repocketed the pencil and drilled two precision holes in less than a minute. He reached out a hand. "Phillips-head screwdriver bit."

"Huh?"

"The little top with an *x* on it."

"You could have just said that." She bent and rummaged through the box. "This?"

"Smaller."

"Ah." She grasped a tinier version. "This one."

"Perfect." Their hands met as she handed him the drill bit and his smile...

Oh, that sweet, crooked smile...

Made her insides flutter. Her breath catch. And because she couldn't breathe or think, she let her fingers linger in his hand for long seconds, their gazes locked.

He winked, grabbed the bit, installed it onto the drill and had two tiny screws in place within seconds. He handed her the drill and said, "Hand up the alarm box."

He was bossy.

So was Haley.

He didn't take orders well.

Neither did she.

"Thank you." He grasped the unit and with one firm twist settled it in place. "I tested the alarm before I came in so I wouldn't wake the boys."

"Good thinking." She waited while he climbed down, then carried the chair back to the kitchen. "But why now? Why at—" she eyed the clock, sighed, groaned and turned "—eleven-fifteen at night?"

"Fires don't read clocks." He tucked his tools back into the case and shrugged into his jacket. "And after last night, I wouldn't have gotten a wink of sleep knowing you might not be fully set up over here. So it was either sleep on your icy, frozen steps in the cold—"

She winced, knowing the steps were treacherous.

"Or head over here and get this done. That way we'd both lose a little sleep, but I figured if it was a shared inconvenience, it wouldn't be that bad."

"Thank you, Brett." She contemplated him, then took a half step forward. "I want you to know I appreciate everything you do."

Her words sounded stiff. He looked instantly uncomfortable, so she closed the rest of the distance between them, determined to have her say. "What I meant to say is that I'm grateful. Trust has never come easy for me. I pull back and that makes things difficult."

"Relationships, you mean."

"Yes."

He mulled her admission, then said, "They don't have to be, Haley."

She paused, then admitted, "I tend to make them that way."

"So stop."

His straightforward gaze said it should be that easy. Haley knew it wasn't, but she nodded and grasped his hand. "I'll try harder. I think the Holy Spirit is giving me a series of wake-up calls in any case. First you, then Maude, then Charlie." She shrugged. "Our own faults are often the hardest to see."

His expression reflected the truth in her words. "I've been a loner all my life."

"In the army?" She let disbelief color her tone. "Neat trick."

"Being surrounded by people doesn't make you less alone," he countered.

Haley knew that firsthand.

"But I don't want to be on the outside looking in anymore. I've already let too much life pass me by."

"You're a hero and a patriot. That doesn't sound like you let too much get by," she protested.

His eyes softened. "Thanks for that, but you know what I mean. You and I have self-protective tendencies that push us apart while there's an attraction that draws us closer."

His accurate assessment only made her heart beat faster. "So… What do we do?"

His smile strengthened her. "See where it goes. As long as neither one of us chickens out."

"I'm not afraid," she told him firmly. And even if she was afraid to take a chance, she made up her mind to conquer the fear because fear was never of God.

"Me either."

"Well, then." She stuck out her hand, feeling a little

silly, but it felt right, too, like they'd just made a pact. "Let's shake on it."

"If that's the best you can do," he told her. The gleam in his hazel eyes said he had other things in mind, but he shook her hand with quiet authority before he picked up his toolbox and moved to the door. "I'll be back in the morning for the boys. We've got a mission to complete and I'm determined that nothing will foil our plan of attack as long as Todd feels better."

"Charlie said he was much better this evening." She followed him to the door, wondering if he might stop and kiss her.

He didn't, and now she wished she'd sealed their agreement in a more personal way, but he turned at the bottom step and gave her a quick salute. "Get some sleep. I'll be back in the morning."

Sleep?

After she'd just spent twenty delightful minutes with a man whose strength and warmth drew her? Haley was certain she wouldn't sleep a wink, but her eyes went to the newly installed smoke alarm as she reached to turn out the light.

He wanted them safe. That small action said more than any sonnet. She fell asleep, more peaceful than she'd been in years.

Chapter Fourteen

A new day, another chance to get a jump on Operation Decoration, but just as Brett aimed for the door to pick up the boys, his mother called.

"Brett?"

"Hi, Mom." He forced calm into his voice. There was no rushing Joanna Stanton. "Do you need a ride today?"

"No."

But she only called when she needed a ride. Which meant… "Have you stopped going to AA?" He didn't add "again," but he thought it.

"No," she replied, surprising him. "Sue Connealy has been driving me. I've gone every day. She's got her five-year pin and she's stable. I decided I wanted to hang around people with more success in the program."

Brett loved the sound of that, but did she mean it this time? "Well, do you need to go shopping? I'd be glad to take you." He didn't add that he was thrilled to talk to her sober, to hear the normalcy in her voice, to touch base with the mother he'd known for so short a time. "After I get the boys, that is."

"Are you watching them today?"

"Yes." He faltered for a moment. Good behavior should be rewarded, but inviting his mother to accompany them? Good idea? Bad? He wasn't sure, but waded in. "I'm taking them shopping for Christmas decorations as long as the little guy's feeling better. He had that stomach bug going around. Would you like to come with us? Help me shop?"

"Really?" She paused. Her breath went unsteady. "That would be all right?"

"I may have directed thousands of troops in my day, but you've got more experience with little boys. I'd enjoy the help."

"Well." The recognition invigorated her voice. "I do love getting things ready for Christmas."

Did she? Brett had no recollection of that, but the past was best left buried. He'd made mistakes of his own. So had she. They both needed to move on. "I'll be over there in about half an hour. And feel free to spend the day with us."

"Okay."

The joy in her tone took Brett back to the few stints of moderation she'd known. Sober, she was lovable. Drunk? Not so much. But if she could turn that corner again, cling to abstinence, well… He'd appreciate the chance to know her that way again.

He took Haley's bumpy steps two at a time a few

minutes later. When she opened the door, he spotted Todd grappling with Tyler on the living room floor. He cocked his head, aimed a smile at the wrestling boys and made a cryptic observation. "Feeling better."

"I don't know how kids do it," Haley answered as she shut the door. "Amazing recuperative powers."

"So it would seem." He shifted his attention to her and tried not to gawk at how pretty she looked. She'd braided her hair. He'd never seen it that way and the pulled-back style accented her heart-shaped face. Those big blue eyes. The softness of her touchable skin.

"You look more rested," she noted, her voice serious. "And I want to thank you again for the smoke alarm."

He grimaced. "It probably seems silly to have come over that late because nothing happened overnight, but—"

"Not silly at all," she told him. She handed off the boys' jackets. "It was nice of you to think of us." Her hesitation said she'd given thought to his actions. "To care about us."

It was his turn to waver. Should he explain his actions? Share the anguish of the previous night? His protective side longed to keep her untouched by danger and darkness, but keeping secrets didn't seem so important anymore. "We fought a bad fire two nights ago."

She nodded, quiet, as the boys wrestled on.

"It was about three hours after we extricated two victims from that bad crash on I-86."

She winced. "Oh, Brett. I heard about that on the radio. They died."

He fought the threatening shadows, knowing their best hadn't been enough to rescue those victims. "Yes. We knew they were bad, but you always hope you've gotten there in time."

She watched him with a quiet look of compassion. A look that said Haley Jennings was strong enough to hear whatever he might have to say. "Four hours later a call came in for a house fire just this side of Birdsall. I was the first one on-scene."

Commiseration filled her eyes.

"We went in after a little boy. A little older than Tyler." He jutted his chin toward the boys. "We got him out before the roof came down, but all the while I kept thinking what would happen to these little guys if there was a fire? An accident? How do parents keep their kids out of danger?" He turned her way more fully. "How could I keep them safe?"

His words might be centered on Todd and Tyler, but Haley knew they reflected the loss of his son, Josiah. She reached out and settled her arms around him in a warm hug. "Life doesn't come with guarantees, Brett."

"I know that." Silence stretched for long moments, but it was a gentle quiet. Soft and peaceful. "I don't ask God for guarantees, but a man likes to know he's got a fighting chance."

"You miss your son."

He stiffened.

"And you don't like to talk about it," she went on, ignoring his reaction. She stayed right where she was, arms around him, her head tucked against his chest, beneath his arm. "I understand that need for privacy even though I surround myself with people to make me feel normal. I push myself to believe that if I just keep doing my best, things will work out." She leaned back and caught his gaze. "I run myself ragged trying to make that happen."

His gaze softened. A crooked smile of acknowledgment made her feel like they'd bridged a small gap. "So I need to talk more and you need to talk less?"

She drew back and poked him. "That's not what I said."

"It's what I inferred. Hey, guys. You ready to go?"

"In a minute!"

"I just have to—"

Brett hauled Todd out of Tyler's grasp. "Knock it off. We've got to hit the road. Stuff to do today. And we're picking up my mother so you've got to be good, okay?"

"The nice l-l-lady wiff the brown hair?" Todd spun his way, an eager smile lighting his face.

"I like her," added Tyler. He zipped his coat, made a face at Todd, called him a slowpoke, then moved toward the door.

"Am not!"

"Are, too. I could zip anything at your age," Tyler

boasted as Todd struggled with the metal fastener. "Coats. Backpacks. Boots."

"I can, too!"

Tyler made a face of disbelief, but kept his silence. His scorn was enough to have Todd reaching out, ready to go another round on the floor. Brett pulled a hat over Todd's ears, hoisted him up and headed out. "On that note, we're out of here. We'll see you tonight. And I know it's Saturday and the co-op will be crazy-busy, but you need to make sure you're covered there for Monday."

"The judge's hearing." She nodded as she slipped into her coat. "I'm on it."

"The whole day," Brett countered.

"But the hearing is in the morning."

"Yes. But it's Monday, and the co-op should be quieter. And remember, people rise to the occasion. If you trust them, they'll earn that trust. Most of them, anyway."

She'd told him last night that she was learning to delegate. She leaned in and kissed the boys goodbye, then glanced up.

Bad move. Brett's expression said he was standing in line, just like his more youthful companions. When she hesitated, he didn't. He swept a soft, sweet kiss to her mouth, stepped back and swung the door wide. "After you."

Would this be what life could be like? she wondered as she walked around the corner toward the co-op entrance. A family, a career, a balance she'd only known in TV movies?

Make-believe, her conscience scolded.

It didn't feel like make-believe. When she was around Brett, windows of opportunity opened, but was she just romanticizing the situation? Possibly. But being in his presence did that to her.

She pulled out her phone to quiet the ring tone, and frowned. A missed call from that same out-of-state number. Once inside the co-op she went into the office and searched the internet for the area code.

Central Arizona.

Haley frowned. She didn't know anyone in Arizona. Not a soul. And sure, it might be a telemarketer, but it wasn't a toll-free number, making that unlikely.

"Haley, good. You're here." Lisa came into the office wearing a Christmas-print florist's apron over a bright red turtleneck. "The Fosters need the back door opened to bring in more antiques."

"I'm on it." She stood and pocketed the keys. "How's your mom today? Any better?"

Lisa's expression said no. "We're on borrowed time. And we knew that, but when the doctor signed the hospice order yesterday, well…" Tears filled her eyes. She blinked them back but not before Haley's filled in sympathy.

"Oh, Lisa." She hugged the other woman.

"I know." Lisa rubbed her sleeve across her face, squared her shoulders and met Haley's look of empathy. "We're as prepared as we can be, but my mother stood by me through everything. My diagnosis, the mastectomy, chemo, radiation. Evan would make an excuse why he couldn't get to the doctor's office. Or the treatment centers. But Mom did. Even with work and the farm, she was always there, always laughing, always joking. And when Evan walked out, Mom's strength and faith helped get me through. I can't imagine life without her, Haley, but I can't stand to see her suffer either."

Haley squeezed Lisa's hand. "You are so blessed to have each other."

"I know." Lisa wiped her eyes one last time. "And my goal right now is to help her every step of the way, which means me here, doing this stuff." She pointed to the greens area by the back door. "So Dad can be home, spending time with her while Adam and Caroline run the Christmas tree side of the farm right now."

Lisa's brother was a New York State Trooper. Time on the family farm wasn't part of his hectic schedule, but right now? He was working nights and helping run the garden center and tree farm part of the business during the day. The holidays were a crankin' busy time for a family-run nursery to deal with illness and death, and Lisa's words prodded Haley.

Lisa and her family delegated the work to make everyone's life easier. While Haley might not have family to help balance her schedule, there was an array of people showing her she wasn't alone, that she had backup as needed. She opened the loading door, shared good-mornings with the Fosters and then hurried back to the ground level, right before she pulled up short.

Water trailed across the floor, pooling around her feet. Alarmed, she pushed open the downstairs bathroom door.

Flooded. And each time someone used the upstairs bathroom, more water gushed forth.

"Uh-oh." Mr. Foster took one look and moved to the utility room to shut off the water.

"Oh, honey." Mrs. Foster stared, round-eyed as the water crept across the tiled floor.

"I've got the mop." Practical and pretty, Lisa maneuvered the rolling mop bucket down the hall. "I've got this. You call the plumber."

Haley pulled out her cell phone and hit the number for the guy who installed her brand-new septic system less than two months before, certain it was going to be a very long day. And when her cell phone buzzed her moments later and her mother's number flashed into the display, she was even more convinced. "Hello."

"Haley."

"Hi, Mom. I'm kind of busy right now, I'm at work. Can I call you back in a little while?"

The aggrieved sigh said no. "I only need a moment. I just wanted to remind you about the annual Christmas ball being held at the club on the seventeenth."

"Because?" For the life of her, Haley couldn't imagine why her mother felt the need to call her attention to the high-brow charity event.

"A lot of good, solid, respectable families will be represented at the ball. Not only could it further your connections…"

Haley was pretty sure that furthering her connections meant an arranged marriage to someone whose fortune and friends would prove advantageous to her mother and stepfather.

"Lots of the young people come home for the holidays."

Score a direct hit on the financial-trading-matchmaking scheme. "Mom, I appreciate the offer of a ticket, but I can't come."

"Why not?"

Haley sighed, knowing the time had come to explain Todd and Tyler's presence. She was equally certain her mother wouldn't understand. "I've got Anthony's two boys living with me."

Silence followed, a thickening quiet, the kind you feel while awaiting imminent disaster. Then, "Why?"

"*Why* do I have the boys?" Haley headed into her office and prayed the septic guy would arrive quickly and give her an excuse to end the call. "Angi passed away last spring and they were with an elderly aunt outside of Trenton."

"They couldn't stay there?"

Breathe, Haley. Breathe.

"Their aunt found Anthony's will that named me guardian."

"Refuse it."

"Mother, I—"

"Haley Monroe Jennings, there is no reason in this world why you should feel the need to take on a half brother's kids, a half brother who never made anything of himself. Like father, like son."

"Anthony died in Afganistan, serving our country," she corrected her mother as she fought rising anger. "He's a hero."

"He joined the service because he couldn't get into a decent college, most likely. I will never understand your desire to surround yourself with people who fail to seize every opportunity they have to better themselves."

"You mean to make more money."

"Romanticize things all you want, Haley. Money makes the world go around."

It wasn't, but she'd been down this road with her mother before. "In any case, I have Anthony's boys and I won't be able to leave them to come to the ball."

"I'll hire a sitter for you."

Haley sighed inside, knowing she'd never approve of the kind of sitter her mother would deem appropriate. "The boys have been through a lot. I'm staying here with them and having a quiet, kid-filled Christmas." Her words were a mockery. She knew that. She hadn't done one thing to prepare for a sweet, quiet Christmas with the boys because her days were filled with work.

"Ted will be very disappointed."

Haley had managed to disappoint her stepfather regularly, so this was nothing new.

"And we're out of town from mid-December until mid-January, so have a nice holiday."

Their leaving was no surprise either. She hadn't had a family Christmas since entering college ten years before. But one way or another, this year she was determined to have a sweet, God-filled, child-centered holy day. "Merry Christmas, Mom."

The soft click said her mother hadn't stayed on the line long enough to hear the good wishes.

The septic system excavator came into the office just then. "I've got the truck out back, we'll troubleshoot this and get you up and running. I think the rain backwashed your tank and caused it to flood. Yours isn't the only system suffering this week."

"But you can fix it?" Haley asked. Begged, actually.

He nodded. "One way or another we'll get it taken care of. And if it needs a pump, we'll install that, no labor charge. No one expects this much rain this time of year, and the amount of business you're doing here means constant use of the plumbing."

"Which is a good thing," Haley told him.

"It is, but I should have done an auxiliary pump from the beginning, because you have to be prepared for the unexpected in business." He waved a hand and headed out back. "I'll let you know when we're up and running. Should be within the hour."

Which brought them to opening time, and that would be a wonderful thing, to have working bathrooms when she unlocked those front doors in forty-five minutes.

* * *

"First, we need this base," Joanna announced. She lifted a round, red-and-green tree holder from the middle of the sprawling seasonal display midmorning. "It's got a nice, deep reservoir. Lots of water keeps the tree healthy."

"Good point," Brett noted. "And how many strings of lights will we need? Two? Three?"

She looked affronted. "Ten."

"That's a thousand lights, Mom." It was Brett's turn to make a face. "Haley's apartment's pretty small, so the tree can't be too big."

"Lights make the tree, Brett. A well-lit tree smiles from within."

"It does, huh?" He didn't recall seeing many smiling trees lately, but if she suggested ten strings, who was he to argue?

"I wuv Christmas twees." Todd pointed to his right. "And I fink I like Christmas twees wiff…"

"With." Brett stressed the "th" sound for the little guy.

Todd puckered and tried again. "Wi-i-th."

"Got it. Good boy."

Todd's smile made Brett feel ten feet tall. "Wots of colors the best."

"Colored lights it is." Brett counted out ten boxes of lights. "Now how about decorations?"

"Well." Joanna led the way to the stacks of decorations, but her expression said she wasn't enamored.

"What are you thinking, Mom?"

"Two things." She smiled at the boys. "We can make some decorations."

Brett pretended shock and fear. The boys laughed. His mother sent him a look of overdone patience until he said, "I'm listening."

"Well, we could take a few pictures of the boys and they could make some of their own ornaments as a gift for Haley. I did this for Sunday school preschoolers about ten years ago and they were easy for the kids to do and the parents just loved them."

Her words reminded him that she'd stayed sober for a decade and a half while he was in the service. She'd probably accomplished a lot in that time frame, so he nodded his encouragement. "I like that idea. What do we need?"

"Canning jar lids, ribbon, glitter, popsicle sticks and glue. And then we'll stop at the Tractor Supply store in Wellsville for some country-themed ornaments."

Country-themed ornaments?

Brett couldn't imagine such a thing.

"And we need a Nativity set." Joanna twined fingers with each little boy and turned them around. "I saw those over here."

Brett had served in multiple nations. He'd spent Christmas on every continent except Antarctica and Australia. He'd seen his share of magnificent Nativity scenes and these boxed sets couldn't compare with the majesty of those, but the light in Todd's and Tyler's eyes as they gently lowered the box holding Mary, Joseph and Jesus into the cart?

Priceless.

"Hey." Tyler tugged Brett's arm. "We need a star, right?"

He pointed to the top of the decorated tree display. "For the top."

"That's a great idea." Brett let Tyler pick out which star would be the most perfect, and smiled when the five-year-old picked out a blue-and-silver star with three dimensional points that lit from within. As they added the star to the cart, Tyler stopped Brett's hand.

"Wait. Can we get her instead?"

He pointed to an angel tree topper toward the back of the display. The angel had soft brown hair. Her pale skin set off deep blue eyes and she was wearing an ivory gown with feathered wings.

Todd stared and gulped. "She's so beautiful."

"She is." Tyler peered up at the angel, then grasped Brett's hand. "I'd rather have her than a star. Really."

Brett exchanged looks with his mother, then nodded. "Sure. Whatever you want, fellas." He hunted for a boxed angel, but couldn't find one. A clerk stopped by and offered his help. When the boys explained their wishes, he offered reassurance, grabbed a stepladder, climbed three rungs and removed the angel topper from the tree. "Looks like this is the last one, sir." He went behind a counter, bent and procured a box. "I can discount it because it's been on display."

"Even better," Brett declared.

The clerk reboxed the angel with care and handed it to Tyler. "Here you go, son."

"Thank you."

"Fank you!" Todd climbed the side of the cart and stretched over the edge to see the angel up close. "She's so pretty."

"She is." Joanna laid a hand on Todd's head. "And you hang on if you're going to ride there, okay?"

"Okay." He beamed up at her, two rows of tiny white teeth showcasing his happiness. Joanna's eyes grew misty, just a little. She turned her gaze up to Brett. "These two are sure easy to love, aren't they?"

Brett couldn't disagree. "I'm kind of fond of them," he teased.

Tyler grinned, smug. "I know you are. We like you, too, Brett."

The big guy's heart dared to open a little more. He knew that children could grow attached easily, especially in Todd and Tyler's circumstances. He didn't want to break their hearts. Let them down. Disappoint them in any way, shape or form. Haley was right in that regard, that they needed to move carefully, putting the boys first.

They stopped at Tractor Supply and bought the ornaments Joanna recommended. As they were checking out, Brett asked, "Mom, do you put up a tree?" It seemed silly not to know that, but she hadn't asked him over since he'd been home and he'd spent the better part of two years in relative seclusion. But those days were gone.

She shook her head.

"Would you like to?" Brett asked. "I'd be glad to help."

Joanna shrugged. "Not much sense in doing it for one person."

Brett understood her reasoning. He hadn't decorated or recognized Christmas in any way other than making donations and helping with the fire department's community projects. And going to church, sitting alone in a back pew, wondering why he'd made the choices he did.

Old news. Move on.

The boys' combined laughter reminded him he'd been moving on, albeit slowly. Until Thanksgiving, that is, when change careened full steam ahead.

They carefully placed the bags of ornaments alongside the lights in the back of the SUV. "And now—" Brett aimed his gaze down "—we get the tree."

"Yes!" Tyler fist-pumped the air.

Todd hugged Brett's leg. "I promise I will l-l-love this tree, Brett!"

Tyler's eyes went wide at the sight of the Greens and Gardens Christmas tree farm a quarter-hour later. Big, beautiful, sprawling spruces and firs filled the grassy lot. A barn wall was hung with wreaths of all styles, from simple to elaborate. Red ribbons danced in the cold wind, a sign that the steady rain might finally turn into snow. Brett and his mother made sure the boys' boots, mittens and hats were fastened snugly before they moved into the forest of pre-cut trees.

The boys stared, round-eyed. "What if we like them all?" Tyler wondered out loud.

Brett grinned, grasped his hand and leaned down. "One will stand out. Talk to us. We'll know for certain that it's the right one because we'll feel so good inside."

"Really?" Tyler turned wide eyes to Brett's.

"I promise."

"Okay." Tyler wriggled his hand free and strode down the rows, a hand cupped to his ear, pausing now and again. He paused before a monster tree and tipped his gaze up, up, up.

"I love it, too, Ty, but it won't fit in Aunt Haley's living room."

"I know." Tyler's eyes swept the massive tree. "But someday I would like to live in a house and have a big ol' tree like this to decorate."

Joanna's winsome smile said she understood the little boy's dream, and their combined looks had Brett imagining all kinds of things. A big living room overlooking the woods. A huge tree, decked out for Christmas. Two little boys playing with model trains and dinosaurs, wearing camouflage clothes and rolling around a soft, thick carpet.

"'We are such stuff as dreams are made on…'" Shakespeare's quote embodied the moment, the look in a little boy's eyes as he allowed himself to dream once more. One way or another, Brett was determined not to let him down.

They found a smaller version of the huge tree,

strapped it to the top of the SUV, stopped for chicken nuggets along the way and got home with plenty of time for naps while Brett and Joanna struggled the tree into its holder and applied the lights. By the time the boys woke up, the tree was ready to decorate.

"But we don't have time to decorate and make the handmade ornaments you suggested," Brett noted to his mother. He lifted the bag of supplies she had him buy.

Joanna attached the bag to the handle of her purse. "We'll make the ornaments another day soon, when Haley's working. Then the boys can wrap them and give them to her for Christmas."

"That's perfect, Mom." Brett smiled down at her, then gave her an impromptu hug, a hug that surprised them both but felt good. Real good. "I couldn't have gotten all this done without your help."

"And the ten strings of lights?" she noted, smiling.

He couldn't deny it. "The tree looks happy."

"Indeed it does. 'I think that I shall never see, a poem as lovely as a tree.'" Joanna smiled as she quoted Joyce Kilmer. Her phrasing resurrected something else. Her love of reading had instilled a similar quality in Brett. He'd forgotten that, but seeing her sober, quoting old poems and wiping little boys' faces made him remember the mother she could have been. And maybe could be again.

"Would you like to stay for supper, Mom?"

She turned, faltered, then shook her head. "Not this time, but thank you. Sue is going to the seven o'clock meeting at the old Oddfellows Lodge hall, so I'm going to tag along. If you can get me home, that is."

"Glad to." He corralled the two excited boys, took his mother back to Wellsville, grabbed bologna for supper and got the boys back to the apartment just before Haley was due to close up the co-op. If everything worked out well, Haley Jennings was about to get the surprise of a lifetime.

Plumbing fixed: Check! And in time for not too much inconvenience. And at no cost because the system was under warranty.

Haley glanced at her watch, saw it was midafternoon and was tempted to run next door to visit Brett and the boys, but the volume of shoppers advised against it.

Moments later, Mrs. Foster sidled up alongside her and touched Haley's arm. "Don't get nervous," she whispered.

Haley's alarm buttons spiked instantaneously.

"And don't look behind you."

Of course she did. And saw nothing.

Mrs. Foster leaned closer. "The other way. To my right. A young woman with a big coat."

Big coats on small people equated shoplifting in a retail establishment, and busy co-ops were easy targets because of the tight exhibit areas, large numbers of small, pocketable display items and throngs of people at holiday time.

Haley swept the row of miniature shops a casual

look. A young woman in a too-big coat stood off to the side of a jewelry display. One hand reached out to stroke the handmade jewelry. Her face softened in appreciation. She lifted the piece, considered it, then set it back down as a look of pain contorted her expression.

Haley rushed forward.

So did Mrs. Foster.

"Come with me," Haley told the young woman. She took her arm and led her to the first-floor office as Mrs. Foster flanked the young woman's other side. "Sit down." Haley bent low, concerned and uncertain. She'd dealt with older folks having spells in Lewisburg, and she'd called the ambulance more than once while working there, but this was a young woman, barely out of her teens. What could possibly be wrong with—

The coat gaped, revealing a very pregnant belly.

Mrs. Foster sighed in commiseration.

Haley drew up a chair alongside the girl. "Honey, are you in labor?"

The girl sighed and gulped. Then she nodded. Fear and despair marked her young features, and Haley had the strongest urge to hug her.

She didn't. "Let's get you to the hospital."

The girl shrank back. "I can't."

"Of course you can," Mrs. Foster announced. "Because that baby's ready to be born."

"No, I can't." The girl put emphasis on the last word. "I have no money, no insurance. I thought it would be all right, but then—" Another wave of pain stopped her, midsentence. Mrs. Foster counted softly as the young woman puffed air, and at that moment Haley would forever count Tina Foster as a new BFF. Left on her own with a young woman in labor, she'd have caved. Tina's presence bolstered her.

"But then?" Haley asked when the pain diminished. By a rough estimate it had been about eight minutes since the last one.

"I tried calling you."

Haley sat back, puzzled. "Me?"

"Yes." The girl nodded, one hand mindlessly twisting a hank of the large coat. "I thought maybe…"

Haley leaned closer. "Do I know you?"

Tears glistened in the girl's dark brown eyes, eyes that reminded Haley of…

"I'm Fiona."

Her father. *Their* father, she corrected herself. Anthony had gotten those dark brown eyes, too. Haley's brain tripped, sighed and dived back into gear as she grasped Fiona's hands. "This is a crazy way to meet, sis."

The tears Fiona had held at bay started flowing. Mrs. Foster cradled an arm around her and handed her a clutch of tissues. "There, there. It will all be fine, just fine. We just need to get you to the hospital, honey, then we'll figure everything out from there."

"But—"

"No buts." Haley gripped her younger sister's hands and stood. "Tina, I'm going to drive her myself. Care to come?" She hoped her eyes showed how much she desperately wanted the older woman's wealth of experience alongside.

"Glad to." Tina flipped open her cell phone. "I'll let Stan and Lisa know where we're off to."

Fiona.

Pregnant.

Here.

Haley was having trouble wrapping her brain around those simple facts. Any help Tina could give was a wonderful blessing.

As they reached the parking lot, indecision paused Haley's steps. Neither Tina nor Fiona would have an easy time crawling into the backseat of her convertible.

"My car." Tina pointed left and jangled a set of keys in her pocket. She hadn't bothered going downstairs for a coat, and the temperature had dropped significantly.

Haley led Fiona across the slick lot, tucked her into the backseat and squeezed her hand as she slid in next to her. "Let's go."

Chapter Fifteen

Surreal. That's how Haley felt as a medical team took turns buzzing in and out of the labor room.

"This is all normal, honey." Tina clasped Haley's hand as Fiona's contractions grew closer, sharper and stronger. "We'll just pray this baby into a safe delivery, you and me."

"Luckily I can pray while Fiona has a death grip on my arm," Haley joked weakly.

"Oh, I'm sorry." Fiona released her hold. Dismay colored an already-blotched face, the efforts of labor making themselves known. "I didn't mean to grip so tight, Haley. Honest."

"She was kidding, dearie." Tina sponged Fiona's face with a cool cloth. "You grab on as tight as you need, but don't tense up. Just relax and breathe. Remember, each contraction brings you a few minutes closer to holding that baby."

Baby.

Reality blindsided Haley. In a few minutes, another

life would join the planet. A new life, tiny. Untarnished. A sweet baby boy or girl, niece or nephew. Unfortunately in their family, messing kids up had become the norm, not the exception.

"Fiona, do we know what the baby is? A boy or a girl?"

She shook her head. Shame clouded her tired eyes. "I went to the clinic early on, but…" She frowned and sighed. "My mother kicked me out. Said I was a disgrace and there wasn't room for me in her new place. That if I was going to make it, I'd have to make it on my own."

Haley's heart went wide. What was it with parents disowning their children? First her father… Then Angi's parents, splitting up and going their own separate ways, leaving Angi with no help following Anthony's death. Her own mother, more concerned with appearance than with substance. Wasn't anything real anymore? Substantial? Grounded in love, rooted in faith?

Brett's face came to her. The gentle, tough, rugged countenance a perfect blend.

But he'd had a child he didn't see, too. A boy who grew up with an absentee father. Did it make a difference that he was serving his country and couldn't see Joe on a regular basis? Or was that a convenient excuse?

A strong contraction twisted Fiona's features. Haley held her hand while Tina called the nurse. From their expression, Haley figured the moment had arrived.

She was right. Within ten minutes a tiny, wriggling,

yowling baby girl was delivered into the waiting arms of a nice medical crew and a very unlikely family.

"Oh." Fiona's eyes filled again as she grasped the baby girl. "Oh, she's so beautiful."

"She is." Haley bent and touched a finger to the softest skin she'd ever known. "Oh, she is, Fiona."

"Does she have a name?" wondered Tina.

Fiona frowned. "No."

"You haven't decided on a name?" Haley asked. "I could get you one of those baby books that list all the names. Would you like one?"

"No." Fiona breathed softly, traced the baby's face with one finger and shook her head. "I can't keep her."

Tina's gaze flew to Haley's. Both women swallowed hard. "You mean, you're giving her up?" Tina sat down with a plunk alongside the bed. "For adoption?"

"Yes."

Haley's brain had misfired at the thought of having her sister suddenly appear and give birth, but to wrap her mind around this new train of thought...

"Fiona, have you thought about this?" She sat opposite Tina and put a hand on her sister's shoulder. "Have you examined all the options?"

"They're precious and few when you're nineteen years old, unmarried and your greatest claim to fame is a cosmetology license from the state of Arizona."

Arizona. The phone calls.

"You were the one who called me with that Arizona number."

Fiona nodded. "I was too afraid to tell you who it

was. Why I was calling. And then this morning I didn't feel well and I was afraid, so I came to Bennington Station, hoping to meet you."

"Well, you accomplished your goal." Haley bent forward and gave Fiona a hug. "Fiona, you and I don't know each other. We may or may not have anything in common, but we are sisters. Being family makes us a unit. And I don't know about you, but all I want now is a normal family experience. Does that make sense to you?"

"Perfectly." Fiona settled a calm gaze on Haley. "Which is why I decided to give the baby up. I've got no one to help me. Her father took off the minute he realized I was pregnant."

Haley winced. So did Tina.

"My mother is busy with her new life in a hippie settlement in Arizona and has no place in her communal life for a daughter and granddaughter." She puffed out a breath. "And I've got no job and no place to stay."

"So you came here."

"Not to beg." Fiona sat up straighter. "I didn't come to mooch off others. I'm not like that, but I couldn't imagine having this baby." She smiled down at the tiny girl in her arms. "Going through labor and delivery." She angled a smile of gratitude toward Tina and Haley. "Alone. And I thought, well…" She paused and shrugged. "You and I had never met. I figured that's just wrong, that two sisters never got a chance to know one another. And Anthony died before I got to meet him and I thought, what if…" She aimed a gaze down to the baby. "If something went wrong, I wanted to at least meet you. See you. It's wrong for family to be kept apart."

Haley's heart warmed to the words, but a niggle of concern urged caution. Fiona had nailed Haley's quandary with her words: They didn't know each other. And she had the boys to consider. Maybe Fiona was the sweet, impetuous young woman she made herself out to be. But what if she wasn't? Could she put the boys at any kind of risk?

No.

But could she stand by and let her sister give up her child without offering to help?

No.

"All right!" A nurse bustled in, smiling, her broad face bright with warmth. "I'm sending this little one down to the nursery to get cleaned up, I'm going to check our young mother here, and then—" she aimed a firm look at Fiona "—you're going to rest, dearie. We'll bring the baby back in a little while, but rest while you can. You're going to need it."

"That's our cue." Tina stood, bent over Fiona and held the younger woman's gaze. "Listen, you aren't the first to have a baby on your own, and you won't be the last, but we've got a nice town here. A great place to settle in and raise this baby. I ain't sayin' it will be easy." She straightened somewhat but kept her eyes on Fiona's. "But it's doable. If you do choose to give this baby up?" Tina let out a sigh. "There's not a thing wrong with that decision either. Lots of parents out there wishing they could hold a miracle like this in their arms." She stroked a finger to the baby's cheek. "Whatever you decide, I want you to know that the folks around here like new blood. Young folks, just startin' out. So you think about that while you pray over this decision, okay?"

"Okay." Fiona's gaze met Tina's and Haley read the longing there, the wish for a gentle, wise mother like Tina. The kind that hangs in for the long haul.

Could she be that kind of mother to Todd and Tyler? Could Fiona do that for this precious baby? Did they dare risk the children's emotional well-being if they were this unsure?

"I'll be back tomorrow," Haley promised. She bent to kiss Fiona's cheek. "And here's my address. I live right behind the co-op." She pressed a piece of paper into Fiona's hand. "My cell is on all the time, so call me if you're worried or concerned or just want to talk, okay?"

"Okay."

They left the nurse with Fiona, but Haley turned back as they approached the elevators. "Maybe I should—"

"Pray." Tina grasped her arm and steered her forward. "Honey, we're coming in on the last chapter of a long, drawn-out play and I can't tell you the ending, but I can tell you this. That little sister of yours needs prayers right now. Prayers for a good decision, prayers for strength, prayers for turning her life around. We know she did good to come here. Seek you out."

They stepped into the elevator and Tina pressed the ground level button.

"But we don't know what's gone before. So we trust, but we proceed with caution."

"I agree." Haley sighed. "But I feel bad, Tina, because I kept meaning to track her down. It kept coming to me, like God was nudging me to find Fiona. Meet her. Get to know her. And I didn't do it."

"We all have those regrets." Tina shrugged. "That's part of life. But right now, you've got a lot on your plate and Fiona isn't sure what she's done, where she's going or what to do. At this point, she needs to act, and we'll react. Ain't no good pushing a woman to keep a child she's not ready for."

Tina's common sense showed the wisdom of her years. Haley reached out and hugged her. "Thank you for finding me in the co-op earlier. For coming to get me when you saw there was a problem."

"You're welcome. And it's been a long time since I attended a birthing," Tina added, smiling. "It was right nice, Haley."

The sight of that newborn, pink, red and mottled. Her lusty cries. Her big eyes, squeezed shut or rounded. Blinking.

A miracle, for sure. "I couldn't agree more, Tina."

Haley was pretty sure nothing could eclipse what she'd just experienced, but when she walked into the Christmas wonderland of her little apartment, she promptly burst into tears.

The boys stared, uncertain.

Brett didn't fare much better.

Their bemused expressions made her smile through the tears.

The half smile broke the impasse. The boys raced for her. Brett stayed where he was as the boys escorted Haley into the decorated living room.

"Brett." She swiped her face with the back of her hands and tried to smile up at him. "This is—" Her eyes welled again.

"Wonderful," he supplied, hopefully. "Our goal was to make you happy…"

"Oh, I am!"

"Women." He angled a look to the boys and squatted low. "They cry when they're happy."

"And when they're sad," Tyler added.

"Mommy cried a wot," Todd went on.

His words pushed Haley to dry her tears. Her overworked emotions were pushing the boys into a past filled with sadness and uncertainty, when her intent was to draw them into a present of love and security. "Well, boys." She accepted a tissue from Brett, wiped her eyes and sat down on the floor. "This is the most beautiful Christmas present I've ever received."

Tyler frowned.

So did Todd.

"But," Tyler began, confused. "Aren't we going to—"

Brett put a finger to his lips. "Remember it's okay to keep good secrets at Christmas, right?"

Todd clapped a hand to his mouth. "That's wight!" he squealed and poked his brother. "We're not 'upposed to tell, Ty."

"I didn't."

"You almost did." Todd settled a serious look of admonishment on his older brother, obviously pleased to call him out.

"Listen, you—"

Todd crawled behind Brett, searching for safety.

"And we're back to normal," Haley breathed, laughing. She hugged Brett's arm and looked around, letting the beauty of the room pull her in. "I'm overwhelmed."

She turned his way and hoped the sincerity of her gaze said more than simple words. "I don't know how to thank you." She stretched and pressed a gentle kiss to his cheek, a kiss that lasted seconds longer than a neighborly peck. A kiss that said she liked the feel of his roughed-up evening skin beneath her lips, the smell of a working man, the joy of close proximity.

His gaze said he got the message, but she read concern in his eyes, too. Concern for her. How could he know her so well after such a short time?

The verdant words of Solomon's Song of Songs filled her. If love was of God, could it be this sweet, this quick, this true? Her family experience said no. Her faithful heart pushed her to become more open.

"Show me everything," she told the boys.

"Well." Tyler took charge and for once, Todd let him. "First we took Brett's mom shopping with us."

"We did?" Haley arched a brow of approval in Brett's direction.

"Mom enjoyed directing us because she has a lot more experience with decorating and shopping and little boys than I do."

"Utilizing resources is the mark of a great leader," Haley teased.

"So we went to the store and we got stuff," Tyler continued.

"Like?" Haley prodded.

"All of it."

"That pretty much sums it up," said Brett. He smiled and palmed Tyler's head. "Of course he's leaving out the best part."

"The Cwistmas twee farm!" Todd jumped up and down, wriggling with glee. "I got to see a bajillion Cwistmas twees, and some of them were blue and we don't like blue trees, do we, Tyler?"

"No."

"Something they agree on," Haley murmured to Brett. "We'll have to remember that."

"For future use," he whispered back, and the word *future* made her think of possibilities she'd thought unrealistic. But right now those options seemed almost tangible.

"We wanted a monster tree," Tyler explained.

"But this apartment is too small." Todd swept the small room a tragic look. "But Bwett said maybe someday we can get a huge tree." His widespread arms added emphasis. "But I fink this twee is really, really nice, don't you, Aunt Haley?"

She didn't hesitate. Stretching to hug both boys she gave them her most sincere, serious look. "I think it's the most beautiful tree I've ever seen. And I love these ornaments." She scooched forward and touched a miniature rustic birdhouse. A wee goldfinch perched in the tiny hole, a twig of greens offering a ledge for ittybitty feet. "They're so precious and country. How did you know I'd love things like this?" she asked Brett.

"Joanna knew." Tyler slid in alongside her and showed her a cotton quilted ornament. The word *JOY* was hand-embroidered on the ornament face. "This one says joy, but they all say different things. Only we got two 'joys' because we want you to be happy about Christmas."

A pang of guilt hit, midsection. "I am happy." She slipped an arm around him, longing to reassure. "And who picked out the angel for the top? She's absolutely beautiful."

"Me." Tyler half whispered the word. He nudged closer to Haley's side and gazed up. His eyes grew moist. His words stumbled, just a little. "She kinda looks like Mommy, doesn't she, Aunt Haley?"

A solid lump reformed in Haley's throat, but she fought it down. "She does, Ty. That pretty brown hair, big blue eyes. Beautiful, just like your mommy."

Todd gazed up, wistful, but then he plopped himself into Haley's lap, alongside his brother. "I fink our mommy would like her."

"Me, too." Haley hugged both boys. "I think it's the best tree ever, guys."

"Exactly what I told them," Brett agreed. "And we were going to make you a special supper, but we ran out of time. Do you like fried bologna?"

She twisted to peer at him. "Can't say I've ever had it, but it sounds delicious."

"I fink I love it so much," Todd whispered up to her. "I didn't fink I'd like it, but Bwett said I should try it, so I did."

"You convinced him." She sent a congratulatory look Brett's way.

He shrugged. "The size difference was a mitigating factor. And I may or may not have threatened his life."

Todd giggled outright. "You're funny, Bwett."

"You, too, my man." He shifted his gaze to the small table they'd moved to the side wall. "Did you guys show Aunt Haley the Nativity scene?"

"The…" Haley turned, saw the aged wood barn and figures and sighed. "I felt so bad this morning, knowing that I used my Nativity set to decorate the co-op and I had done nothing here for the boys. I don't know how to thank you."

"I might think of a way." His grin and wink held warmth and promise. A warmth she'd never felt before. "We'll discuss that later. Right now I'm going to make you a sandwich while the boys put their pajamas on."

"Do we have to?"

"Now?"

"Yes and yes." He pointed toward the bedroom. "Go."

"All right." They trudged off and Haley followed Brett into the kitchen.

"They listened."

He grinned as he heated the small frying pan. "This time." He cut into the edges of two pieces of thick bologna and settled them into the hot pan. "This takes only two minutes, but you can use those two minutes to tell me what upset you today."

"That obvious?"

He shrugged. "Maybe not to everyone. But to me?" He put mustard on two slices of bread and turned. "Yes."

"It's too long to go into right now, but I got a surprise visitor at the co-op today. A younger sister I'd never met. From my father's third failed marriage."

"Aha." Brett turned the bologna before shifting a look her way. "It didn't go well?"

"There's the question of the hour," Haley answered. "I found a sister and delivered a newborn niece in the space of four hours."

"Say what?" Brett frowned at the pan, turned the hot bologna out onto the fresh bread and slapped the sandwich together with a deli man's finesse. "Tell me you're kidding."

"The miracle of life, a new sister who may or may not be sincerely sweet and wanting to do the right thing and a baby who may be given up for adoption. Who could make that up?"

Brett put the sandwich in front of her and sank into the adjacent chair. "This all happened today?"

"Within the last five hours."

"Haley." He put a big hand on hers. "She's all right? The baby's all right?"

"Fine. Tina Foster went to the hospital with me. We were the birth coaches." His expression of disbelief almost made her sputter. "Hey, I did just fine, I'll have you know. When I wasn't fighting nausea."

He laughed out loud, but his grip said he commiserated. "What a day. We'll talk later," he added as the boys trooped out. Todd had Panther clutched tight to his chest, but Haley noted a difference instantly.

"Panther has pajamas?"

"Cwistmas pj's," confirmed Todd. He held the scruffy cat up. "Bwett saw these in the store and he figured we could match." While the plaids were slightly different, the red, gold and black color scheme was similar.

"I love them," she declared.

Todd's grin said he agreed. Tyler asked, "Can we watch TV now?"

Brett shook his head, gave Haley's arm a squeeze of reassurance and stood. "Nope, we're going to read two of those new books we got today, and then bedtime."

"But…"

"But!"

"No buts." He tapped his watch. "Church in the morning and you boys need to get up and get moving when Aunt Haley calls you. The first time," he added in his tough voice.

"Okay."

"We will."

"And that way you might be able to make it to Good Shepherd in time for the nine o'clock service." Brett added the aside to Haley.

Mouth full, she waved her sandwich in affirmation.

By the time the boys were tucked into bed after stories, bathroom and teeth brushing, Haley was ready for a good night's sleep herself, but she needed to share the day's crazy journey with Brett.

She closed the bedroom door with a gentle click and sank into the one and only chair. "So, do you think God forgives us when he nudges us to do nice things and we ignore him?"

Brett pondered her words, unsure where she was going. He'd been on the flip side of that question for years, and he had no answers, but he'd promised God he'd move beyond. "Always."

"Hmm." Haley frowned, drew up her knees and wrapped her arms around them. "I've been meaning to search for Fiona and get to know her ever since I graduated from Bucknell. I didn't do it. And I barely stayed in touch with Anthony, and now he's gone. Maybe if I'd been a better sister to Fiona, she'd have chosen more wisely. I feel like God was pushing me to find her, and I ignored Him. How do you explain dissing God?"

Brett spread his hands. "You apologize and move on."

"That easy?" She turned a troubled gaze to him. "I've had ten years as an adult to get to know her. I should have tried harder."

He stood, crossed the room and crouched by her side. "Plenty of time yet. She sought you out. The baby is healthy. And whatever she decides, we'll offer her love and support."

"We?"

He nodded, stood and pulled her up from the chair. "This town takes care of its own. Always has. Always will. I didn't always see that," he admitted. "And I've spent years wishing I'd spent more time with Josiah before he died, so I get what you're saying. But from now on, we face forward. And I'll let Charlie and LuAnn know about Fiona." When Haley frowned, he went on, "Charlie and LuAnn did foster care for years. And they've had more than one unwed mother in their care. If Fiona wants to stay, I'll see if Charlie and LuAnn can offer their spare room."

"Really?"

Her expression said he'd come through looking like a hero multiple times that night. He liked that reaction. He grinned, tweaked her nose and moved toward the door. "Yes, but let's see if your sister is willing to stay. She might not be ready to put down roots."

"She has a child, a daughter," Haley protested.

Brett grimaced. "That's not always enough, Haley." Her expression said she agreed but didn't like it. Neither did he. He sandwiched her hands between his and jutted his chin toward the living room beyond. "Pretty good tree, huh?"

She smiled back. "The best."

"And the Nativity scene?"

"So beautiful."

He drew her closer. "The boys loved doing this for you."

"Did they?" She had to arch back to see him, and that made her kissably close.

"Mmm-hmm." He bent down and feathered a gentle kiss to her mouth, her cheek and then just held her for long seconds, enfolded in his arms, tucked against his ribs. "Me, too."

"Thank you."

"You're welcome." He kissed the top of her head, released her and opened the door. "I'll see you tomorrow afternoon. I'll keep the boys while you work and if you want to go see Fiona before the co-op opens, I'll grab them early."

"You're not too busy?"

He grinned, realizing that maybe this was what God had in mind all the while, that Haley would come here, needing love, short on time and funds with two tiny souls depending on her. What better match for that than a big, strong soldier with a growing business, money in the bank and a searching heart, just like hers? "Not at all."

"Wonderful."

His smile said he agreed. "See you tomorrow." The half circle of light from her door followed him through thickly falling snow. As the arch thinned and faded, he mentally acknowledged his growing feelings. He hated to leave her. Hated to walk away at night, when what he longed for was a home and family. A fireplace for cozy nights with Derringer and the boys tumbling around a spacious room. To be with Haley, come home to Haley.

Or have her come home to him. That painted a more realistic picture.

Was he misreading the signs? He didn't think so, but he knew she needed time. As far as he knew, it was his to give.

Chapter Sixteen

Petition for Legal Guardianship Granted.

Haley held the stamped official document up as she and Brett led the boys out of the county office building in Belmont on Monday morning. "It's done!"

"It is." Brett grabbed up Tyler and swung him around. "Tomorrow we get checked by the doctor, and then Wednesday you get to start school." He ignored the hint of fear he saw in the five-year-old's eyes. "But for today?" Brett tipped his head back and let snowflakes land on his face. "We play."

"Play?"

"Play?" echoed Todd.

"Yup. We're going to celebrate by eating good food and going sledding."

Excitement brightened Tyler's face. "I've never been sledding!"

"Ever?" Brett drew back, amazed. "Really?"

"Really."

"Around here sledding is not only enjoyed, it's

pretty much expected for a good three months of the year," Brett explained. "Let's go home and get you guys dressed...."

"And ourselves." Haley noted the skirt and stockings she'd set off with a tall pair of high-heeled boots with a quick glance. Boots that had drawn Brett's attention more than once. "I've got some old boots stuffed in the back of my closet."

"And layers," Brett advised.

She gave him a quick salute. "Yes, sir. Do we have sleds?"

"Borrowed from LuAnn and Charlie," he assured her. Once they got the boys strapped into their car seats, he gripped Haley's shoulders. "How does it feel?"

She breathed out a sigh of relief. "Like I'm not in limbo anymore. Like we're moving forward." She jerked her head toward the beautiful, historic county office building. "But a little part of me wonders if that nice judge has a clue what he just approved."

Brett laughed and hugged her. "I wish you had as much faith in yourself as others do."

"You're right." She pulled back and stuck that cute chin into the air. "Enough with the self-doubt. Let's go get bundled up and have fun."

"I'm with you."

His words inspired one of those special smiles, the kind that held hope aloft. They grabbed a celebratory breakfast at the Black-Eyed Susan Café, then headed for the Bald Mountain hills on Buehrings Road once they'd dressed in proper gear.

"Brett." The awed look on Haley's face said she loved the picturesque hillside setting as she helped Todd out of the car. Brett couldn't disagree. Open land, dotted with trees, rose to thickly forested state park lands above them. Todd's thick boots hit the deepening snow and he tumbled, face first.

"Oh, honey!" Haley reached to grab him, but Brett beat her to it.

"Got him." He dusted the snow off, swiped Todd's scarf across his rosy cheeks and set him back down. "Go slow, little man. It's getting deep. You need to get a feel for it."

"I love this!" Tyler bragged as he raced up the hill, his longer legs making light work of the snow.

Haley's phone buzzed. She glanced at the readout, ignored Brett's frown and answered. "LuAnn, how's everything going?"

Brett couldn't hear LuAnn's end of the conversation, but Haley's part told him that Fiona would be going home with Charlie and LuAnn, at least long enough to examine her options.

"Tell them we'll stop by later so Fiona and Reilly can meet the boys."

Haley repeated his words, said goodbye, then frowned. "Should we be there, helping them?"

"Helping them what?"

"Get Fiona settled."

Brett angled a look to the two whooping, shrieking boys. "A lot of help we'd be."

"I guess," she answered, chagrined. "It feels like I'm passing the buck, having others take over."

"You think too much." Brett hauled out the sleds. "Charlie and LuAnn will love doing this, and if Fiona stays, Reilly and Shelby might grow up to be best friends forever because Jess is only a few blocks away. Stop trying to control the world."

"I will," she promised. She grabbed a sled and followed the boys uphill. "And listen, old-timer, if you need help getting up here—" she shot him an over-the-shoulder grin "—I can slow my steps a little."

"You'll regret those words soon enough, Haley."

"You think?"

A saucy laugh drifted down to him, but Brett hadn't spent the last twenty years at a desk. He cruised by her with the sled held over his head and shouted back, "Not think. Know." He got to the crest of the hill, snugged the two boys onto the sled between his knees, and sailed downward before she'd made it up the first time. The boys' screams of delight mingled with her bemused smile to make this a day to remember.

Charlie referred to times like this as "make a memory" days, those times when he and LuAnn would gather the newest generation around them and do simple things. Right now Brett could envision a lifetime of make-a-memory days, right here on the south slope of Bald Mountain.

＊ ＊ ＊

Haley couldn't remember a better day. Brett had brought along a man-sized thermos filled with hot chocolate and marshmallows, and when the boys tasted the creamy, melted mix an hour later, their eyes grew wide. "Oh, this is so good, Bwett."

"Br-r-r-ett," Haley reminded Todd.

"Brrrrrett!" Todd tried again and half growled the *r*.

Brett grinned and shoulder-nudged the little guy. "That was perfect. You sounded like a pirate."

Todd beamed. Even Tyler smiled at his success, and the boys looked adorable, perched on the hood of Brett's SUV.

"So, boys." Haley decided a direct approach was best. "We're going to meet your Aunt Fiona later today and your new baby cousin, Reilly."

"Huh?"

"We have a cousin?"

"You do," she continued. "She's a tiny baby—"

"Like Jesus!" Tyler shouted, delighted.

"Yes. And we can't touch her yet because she's so little, but I want you to meet your aunt Fiona. Your dad, Fiona and I were brother and sisters."

"Where did you live?" Tyler wondered.

"All over," Haley told him. Simple, she decided, was better. "But Fiona is here now and she wants to meet you guys."

Todd's eyes went round. He exchanged a look with Tyler and both boys looked suddenly concerned. Glum, in fact.

"Hey, what's wrong?" Brett put an arm around Tyler and bent low. "What's up, my man?"

"She might take us away."

Todd wiggled closer to Haley's side. "To somepwace else and we don't want to go somepwace else. We want to stay wiff you guys, forever."

"Oh, honey." Haley wrapped Todd into a hug. "No one's taking you away. Remember what that nice judge said this morning?"

"Have a good day?"

"Before that," Haley reminded them. "He said that I could take care of you until you grow up."

"As big as Brett?"

"Yes," she promised.

"And I'll be here," Brett pledged. "And Charlie and LuAnn and the guys at the store and the friends you'll make at school."

"So we really get to stay." Tyler's steadfast gaze said he wanted no games. "And be kinda like your little boys?"

"Yes." Haley hugged them both, careful not to spill their drinks. "We're a family now."

Mollified, Tyler pointed east. "Can we go see that barn? It's really cool."

"Sure." Brett stowed the empty cups into the back of the car and hoisted Todd onto his shoulders. "I love classic barns."

Haley smiled up at him. "I do, too. I have a collection of barn calendars from a vendor in Lewisburg. I kept them just for the pictures. Barns are so—" she shrugged "—country. Rustic. And big." She laughed as they drew closer.

The classic horse barn appeared to have rooms upstairs. Twin windows faced the wide, curving drive leading up to the barn. The high-pitched roof with two small dormers facing south gave the upstairs a homey feel, while the first level was clearly a stable.

"Did Jesus get born in a barn like this?" Tyler asked.

Brett shook his head. "No. They didn't have a lot of wood in Bethlehem. Not too many trees. Their stables were mostly in nice, warm caves."

"I fink I like this better," Todd declared. "It's huge."

"Oh, it is." Haley laughed and plowed through the snow to peer into the windows. "Post and beam construction. And in such fine shape."

"A good roof," Brett told her. He pointed up. "Weather won't hurt a barn as long as it's got a good roof, and this classic metal roof will last for decades."

"It's beautiful, right?" Haley turned and smiled at him. "Don't tell me I'm crazy for thinking so because I can just see this sweet old barn turned into a house. Shutters on those windows." She pointed to her right. "And on the front. The crossbuck doors are just the perfect country touch. And so much room."

Brett had no trouble seeing her vision. Imagining the gracious old barn turned into a solid, stable family home. A place where kids and dogs could run free and explore. Trees, animals and a pond on the other side, closer to the road, with a state forest preserve just above them. Safety and solitude, all in one.

"Where's the house?" Todd asked.

Brett pointed north. "The original house is up there. The family went broke when industry moved out of this area, and they lost the place. It's been for sale for years."

"How sad." Haley pressed her lips into a thin line. "I hate to think of places sitting empty. Lonely."

Tyler made a face. "Houses don't get lonely, Aunt Haley. They're not people."

"That's right," Brett told him, but he wondered at the same time. An empty house did seem sad, but a broad-based barn, restructured to fit the needs of a growing family...

"Hey, guys." Haley interrupted his thoughts with a wave of her cell phone. "LuAnn just texted me that they're home and all is well. Why don't we go home, get cleaned up, have a quick rest and go see that new aunt and baby cousin?"

"Okay!"

"I'll race you, Todd!"

Brett knew an unfair advantage when he saw one, so he re-planted Todd onto his shoulders and raced Tyler to the car. When he won, Tyler scowled. "I don't think that's fair."

"Neither is taking off with a head start on a little brother," Brett replied. "Hop in, Ty. Let's head home."

The older boy didn't frown at the word *home* like he had those first days, and Brett saw that as a good sign. Slowly but surely the boys were planting roots in Allegany County.

"She's so tiny." Tyler's eyes went wide as he gazed at little Reilly Jennings a few hours later. "Can she break?"

Fiona sent him a sweet smile of commiseration. "I think so. That's why I'm being extra careful."

Tyler angled her a "better you than me" look. "Can I play with her when she gets bigger?"

Haley watched Fiona struggle with that question. In the end, she shrugged. "I don't know. We'll have to wait and see, okay?"

"Sure." Tyler agreed with all the innocence of youth.

Brett strode in with Todd after a quick bathroom run. "Just look, okay, buddy? Don't touch her. She's too tiny."

LuAnn led Todd closer. "This is your aunt Fiona and your cousin Reilly."

Todd's mouth went round. He leaned up to Fiona and gave her a sweet, little-guy kiss on the cheek. "I am so glad to know you and your baby! I always wanted a baby around."

"Oh, you darling." Fiona's eyes went moist. She swiped a hand against them as the baby started to fuss in her arms.

"Feeding time," LuAnn announced. Her cheery voice said it was time for the boys to leave the room as she handed Fiona a nursing cape. "Charlie's got cookies in the kitchen, boys. And you'll get to see Reilly again soon."

They might have been enchanted by the wonder of a baby, but the boys loved the reality of LuAnn's homemade cookies. They raced to the kitchen at the back of the house.

"Anthony's boys." Fiona sighed, rearranged the baby beneath the cape and met Haley's gaze. "I'm so happy to have met them, Haley. They're beautiful. And it's amazing that you've taken them on like you have."

"Oh, I have help." Haley aimed a smile of gratitude toward LuAnn. "Between Brett and Charlie and LuAnn and other folks in town, people step up to the plate all the time. And if you decide to stay, Fiona?" Haley shifted her attention back to the young nursing mother. "I'll do everything I can to help you, because that's what families should do."

Fiona's gaze tightened. "That's not a familiar scenario, Haley."

"Not to me, either," Haley answered. "But do you remember the prayer that says, 'let peace begin with me, let this be the moment now...'"

"I've heard that."

"That's how I see our family," Haley told her. "That if we—" she waved a hand between herself and Fiona "—change the way we look at family and commitments and faith, we add a little more goodness to the world."

"And that's why you took the boys."

Haley shrugged. "Kids don't ask to be born, but

each one is a sweet miracle." She smiled at her younger sister. "Until they start sassing, of course."

LuAnn laughed.

Fiona smiled. "I'm so glad I came here."

Haley's moment of truth had arrived. She moved forward and knelt down alongside her sister's chair. "And I'm sorry it came to that. I should have gone looking for you. Found you. I'm the older sister and it was up to me to come to you and I didn't do it, even though I felt like God was nudging me along. Prodding me. Can you forgive me, Fee? Please?"

Fiona's eyes filled with tears. She reached out her free arm and draped it around Haley. "We've got each other now. And that's what matters, right?"

"Yes." Haley sat back, mopped her eyes and sighed. "And now that we've started a cry fest, I need to get those boys home, cleaned up and into bed."

"Good night, Haley. And Brett, it was nice to meet you," she called softly.

"Glad to have you here, Fiona." Brett's voice came back from across the small living room.

She sent Haley and LuAnn a smile that seemed a little more relaxed. "It's good to be here."

The thought of the young, single mother sent Brett backward in time.

He'd gone off to the service, leaving Deb alone and pregnant. He'd rationalized it as a young man, that the service would provide enough money to help raise a child, but what he saw tonight…

The wanting look in a young woman's eyes…

Said he'd done an awful job of taking care of things. He called Deb, and asked if he could swing by her place once Haley and the boys were home.

"Now?"

He imagined her looking at the hour, knowing he wouldn't arrive until after nine o'clock that night. "Yes, if that's okay."

She didn't quibble or hesitate. Instead she said, "I'll put the coffee on. Head on down."

When he got there, a man was waiting with her. "Brett, this is my fiancé, Peter."

Peter stretched out a hand, but his gaze said Brett's impromptu visit made him curious. And maybe a little protective.

"Have a seat." Deb waved a hand toward the table, grabbed the pot and filled a mug. "Still black?"

"Yes."

"There you go." She sat alongside Peter and faced Brett. "What's going on?"

Direct as always. Brett paused, then dived in. "I came to apologize."

"For?" Deb's expression questioned his intent.

"Leaving you to raise Josiah alone."

She sat back, surprised. "Explain."

Wasn't admitting it enough? Obviously not. He hunched forward, his hands wrapped around the warm mug. "I did the unthinkable. I created a child with you and then joined the service and left you all alone."

Deb tapped one finger onto the table. "Is this because you think I did a bad job raising Joe?"

"No, no, not at all." Brett sat upright, wondering how she could think that. "He was amazing. Wonderful. I just feel like a first-class jerk for never being around, never giving him a dad to be with."

"Ah." Brows drawn, Deb considered his admission. For drawn-out seconds she looked uncomfortable, then made a little face of consternation and admitted, "I was kind of glad you weren't around, Brett."

He pulled back, affronted.

"Now, don't go getting all military on me. Let me explain." She paused, choosing her words with care. "We weren't going to get married, right?"

"No." He'd asked, she'd refused, end of story.

"And all around me there were young mothers with babies who were going through all kinds of drama with their ex-husbands or boyfriends. It seemed epidemic at the time, and all I could think of was how lucky I was that you trusted me to raise Joe to be a fine young man and sent money like clockwork. Brett—" she leaned forward and covered one of his hands with one of hers "—I loved that boy, heart and soul. And I loved that you entrusted him to me. Sure, he missed some things because you were gone, but you know what?"

He shrugged, mystified that she saw this so differently.

"I told him that his father provided for him. That his father was a brave, heroic soldier. He had copies of every one of your advancements and commendations because those are important, Brett. He kept every one of the letters and cards you sent. I wanted him to be a strong, solid citizen like his father. And he was." She shook her head at him. "Never in my life did I think of you as a deadbeat dad because your job took you away."

Relief blanketed him, the soothing emollient of forgiveness. Not hers. His. "You didn't hate me?"

She laughed. "No. How silly of you to think that. I was free to live my life, create a career and raise Joe the way I wanted because you provided for him each and every month. Do you know how rare that is?"

He didn't, but he was glad she saw the upside of the half-full glass.

She grabbed Peter's hand. "Peter and I are getting married next month. I'm forty-two years old and I'm planning to start a family." She smiled at his look of surprise and went on, "So I suggest that if God has sent you a new opportunity at this point in your life, quit beating yourself up and go for it. Second chances are amazing things."

They were. He took a long sip of his coffee, and finished what he came for. "I'm sorry I didn't come to the funeral."

Her face shadowed. "I was sorry, too. I would have liked for you to be there."

Brett fought the rise of emotion in his chest, his throat. "I couldn't forgive myself for his death. If he hadn't followed me into the service…"

"Brett, there's one thing you should know." This time the tap of her finger was stronger. More insistent.

"Josiah Stanton followed no one. Ever. He was his own man from the time he was a little boy. He chose the service because it felt right to him. He prayed on it, studied his options and then went for it, full tilt, just like his father. But not because you did it first," she assured him. "He did it because he was so much like you. And that was never a bad thing, Brett. I considered it a blessing."

Her heartfelt words made it harder to fight back his emotions. He stood.

So did she and Peter.

Brett reached out and gave her a hug. "Thank you."

"Back at ya."

He reached out a hand to Peter. "Congratulations to both of you."

"Thanks." Peter shook the offered hand and then put an arm around Deb's shoulders. "Good to meet you, Colonel."

No one had used his rank since Joe's death, but tonight, coming from this man, it sounded all right. Brett nodded. "Good to meet you, too. And good luck with—" he aimed a smile at Deb "—everything."

She met his smile with one of her own. "You, too. And if there's a wedding involved, I wouldn't say no to an invitation."

A wedding. Hers. His.

The idea of a forever-after with Haley seemed so clear. Sure, they needed to get to know each other better, and the boys needed time to settle in, but in his heart, nothing had ever felt this right before. He gave them a nod and a quick salute. "Will do. Good night."

"Good night, Brett."

The snow had stopped falling, but the hush of the night, last week's slush now blanketed in pale, pristine white, made everything seem washed clean. The Psalms spoke of a clean heart, a faithful spirit. Tonight, Brett felt that sweet Psalm to the core of his being.

Chapter Seventeen

"I'm too scared," Tyler whined as Haley pulled up to the school building early Wednesday morning. "What if nobody likes me?"

"Why wouldn't they like you?" Haley shut off the engine and decided not to elongate this parting. She'd keep it short and sweet. Then she could cry all the way back to Bennington Station because Tyler was sure to be upset. "Got your backpack?"

"Yes." Chin down, Tyler dragged each step toward the school.

Patience, Haley. Give him time to adjust. Except the last thing she had today was time, but at least Brett had Todd cared for. A security guard waved her toward the main office, and Haley had a hard time slowing her steps to match Tyler's. By the time she pushed open the office door, Tyler's face had gone sullen and silent.

That did not bode well for anyone.

Keeping her head up, Haley smiled at the secretary

she'd met last week and handed over a folder. "Guardianship, vaccinations and physical records."

"Excellent." The woman's smile said she read the situation accurately. "Well, if you don't mind, Miss Jennings, I'm going to take Tyler to his classroom right now. He's just in time to help with Hector the Gila Monster."

Tyler's eyebrows perked. "You guys have a Gila monster?"

The secretary pretended surprise. "Doesn't every school?"

Tyler looked befuddled. "I don't know."

"Well." She reached for his hand matter-of-factly. "I can't vouch for others, but not only does Mrs. Ambrose have a Gila monster, but she also has a skink lizard, two black-and-white teddy bear guinea pigs and an aquarium."

"Really?"

"Oh, yes." She bent to Ty's level. "You didn't know this? Really?"

"No." Ty's sincerity said this was news to him. "I thought she'd just have, well… other kids in there."

"Those, too." The older woman's eyes indicated Haley could head for the door. "He's on bus sixty-one this afternoon."

"And we'll be waiting for him," Haley assured her.

She'd expected reluctance. Maybe even resistance. But as the soft-spoken secretary made her way down the hall, Ty's hand clasped in hers, he didn't even give Haley so much as a backward glance.

Which was strangely disappointing and a big relief all at once. By the time the weekend came with the influx of customers and tourists brought by the Christkindl Market Fair up and down Main Street and in the Park Round, Haley was starting to feel more sure of herself and the daily schedule.

Todd loved being Brett's right-hand man. The pair would pop into the co-op now and again, just to tell her what they'd done or what they hoped to do while Tyler was in school.

It was adorable on both parts.

By day two Tyler decided he loved school and that Mrs. Ambrose knew more than any adult on the planet. Haley crossed "Help Tyler adjust to new school" off her to-do list.

Nice weather helped the Saturday fair be typically busy, with crowded streets and customer-filled stores and booths. Large white tents filled the Park Round, with big heaters blasting warm air into the canvas walls. The co-op had enjoyed thriving business all day. While Tyler was old enough to help Brett by taking tickets in the firemen's chicken-and-biscuits booth, Todd stayed with Charlie, LuAnn, Fiona and Reilly. By four o'clock, Haley knew Charlie and LuAnn could use a break, the shops were well-manned and she needed to spend some time with the boys. She turned the keys over to Maude, went to Charlie and LuAnn's through the back roads, admired baby Reilly, hugged Fiona and tucked Todd into his car seat just before dusk.

"Hey, we might be able to see the park lights come on from the car."

Todd craned his neck up. "I don't see any."

"When we get closer," Haley promised. "I'll let you know. They'll hit the switch in a few minutes, because it's just getting dark."

"I wuv Cwistmas wights!"

"I l-l-love Christmas l-l-lights," she corrected him.

"Me, too!" He aimed a big grin through the rear-view mirror. "Me and you both like them a lot!"

"Hey." She made a face back at him. "You said that perfectly. Have you been practicing?"

He dimpled. "Me and Br-r-rett practice all the time. He says I'm very smart."

"He's absolutely right." A call came through her hands-free phone. She saw Maude's number and answered. "Maude, what's up? Problem?"

"We can't get the drawer open, Haley." Maude sounded as if she really didn't want to be bothering Haley, but not being able to give people change was rather important. "It's stuck before, but never this badly."

Haley mentally scolded herself.

She must have given them the old key. She'd had a new one made because the older one didn't fit cleanly and a new key was way less expensive than a whole new cash register. "I've got the good key with me, Maude. I'll be right there."

"Sorry, dear."

"No problem. Todd and I are just around the corner anyway."

She pulled into a parking space, helped Todd out of his seat, grasped his hand and headed for the door.

Todd planted his two feet and stopped dead. "Do you have to work again?"

"No." Haley shook her head at him. "I just have to give this key to Mrs. McGinnity."

"Why?"

"Because the one they have is broken," she explained.

"I want to see the lights." His lower lip thrust out. His cheeks puffed. His body suddenly weighed three times its normal weight when she tried to lift him to move the last few feet into the co-op.

"We'll climb up to the second floor and see the lights, okay? When they come on," she promised. "But not if you don't behave. I've just got to give Maude this key—"

"And go to stupid old work again."

"No." She bent and looked him right in the face. "I'm done working, but I do need to drop this off. And being mean to me isn't going to get you anywhere. My work isn't stupid. It's nice. I like my job a lot."

"Probally better than you like us," scolded Todd.

"That's not true."

"Well, you don't spend any time wiff us, and all your time over here."

That part was true. How she wished it weren't.

"Todd, please. Just let me drop this off and you've got me the rest of the evening."

He thrust his lower lip out farther and stomped his way into the co-op, making sure everyone heard and saw his discontent. Haley saw a few looks of empathy from other women, but kept her eyes trained ahead. She'd get this done, then torture the little monster at home for embarrassing her in public.

That thought made her feel much better.

"Haley, do you have a minute?" Tina Foster waved her down right after she handed the key to Maude.

"I don't, not really," Haley called back, but Tina had been so helpful during Reilly's birth that Haley couldn't really say no. She took a half-dozen steps down the hall and said, "I've got like ten seconds. Todd's having a fit because I stopped at all and I've got to get him home and settled down. He's in one of those moods."

"You go on, then," Tina told her. "I just wanted your opinion on this." She held up two beautiful baby dresses, one white, one ivory. "For Reilly. Which do you think would be better?"

"Oh, they're both so beautiful, Tina." Haley fingered one, then the other. "I'd say the white."

"White it is." Tina set the ivory gown back on the counter. "I'll drop it by tomorrow."

"Excellent." Haley turned, stretched out a hand for Todd, and got nothing but thin air. "Todd? Todd?" She raised her voice the second time, knowing she was drawing attention to herself, but not caring. "Todd, where are you?"

No answer came. The crowds had thinned in the past hour, but there were still enough people to make a disappearing trick pretty easy for a three-year-old.

"I'll help you." Tina bustled out from behind her counter. "I'll go this way. You head back toward the front."

The front.

Outside.

The lights.

Haley ran, but her heart was in her throat. She'd promised he could see the lights turn on. And she'd broken that promise when he was overwrought and tired from a busy day.

Why hadn't she clung to his hand? Why did she expect a three-year-old to stay still when she knew better?

A scream from the parking lot hiked her adrenaline, but even before she got through the door, she knew.

Oh, she knew.

Lights careened every which way as cars skidded to a halt. Metal crunched metal. The sound of breaking glass split the night. And in the middle of it all a tiny boy lay sprawled, face-down, opposing headlights bathing his still, blue-clad body with light.

Haley didn't know she was screaming until someone grabbed her.

A customer darted around her and raced to Todd's side. "I'm Dr. Eber from Olean. Step back. Step back, please."

Sirens sounded from down the road, but Haley knew the exit traffic from the festival might delay the ambulance long minutes.

She didn't count on Brett. He was there in record time, clearing the way for the ambulance to pull up close. "We've got head trauma, a possible broken arm and his breathing is shallow," the doctor reported as the medics bent close.

Fear froze Haley's heart.

"Thanks, Doc." The EMT began preparations for stabilizing Todd's head and spine for transport. Gentle hands turned the little boy. Sharp scissors sliced through the new, blue coat. The sight of the coat falling open and blood on Todd's favorite superhero shirt did her in.

"Oh, God. Oh, God, please don't take him. Please help him to be okay. Please…"

"I've got you." Brett's arms closed around her.

She pushed away. "No. Go help him!"

"I can't, Haley. We've got to trust them to do their jobs, to take care of him. Come on, let's get you in the ambulance. You can go with him."

She wanted to hit something. Anything. She wanted to take years of business-first frustration out on someone. Unfortunately, Brett was in the line of fire. "Don't patronize me, Brett. We both knew I wasn't capable of taking care of kids. We saw that from the beginning. And now…" A sob wrenched free from a deep-set corner of her heart.

Brett set firm hands on her shoulders. "He'll be fine,

Haley. And what he needs right now is for you to pull yourself together. Do you understand me?"

Brett's face looked stern. Impassioned. Angry.

Well, he had every right to be. He'd kept these boys safe and sound for weeks on end, and the first afternoon she stepped up to the plate, her sweet little boy was lying hurt and unconscious on cold, wet asphalt.

But this wasn't the time or place for hysterics. She hauled in a deep breath, crawled into the ambulance alongside the too-big gurney, and set her mouth in a grim line.

She'd suck it up for the night because she had to, but come Monday morning she'd march into that courtroom, tell the judge what he could do with his vote of confidence and walk swiftly away because this very afternoon she saw the image of her mother, the money-first, managing control-freak side she abhorred.

Only today she saw it in herself.

Chapter Eighteen

The fifteen-minute drive to Allegany Community Hospital seemed to take hours. Brett gripped the wheel, wondering if Todd would be all right. A car versus a three-year-old?

Fear put a grip on his soul.

In a parking lot. Going slow. Don't jump to worst-case scenario.

Brett didn't do that in general, but this time his heart was involved. He remembered the contractor's confession from two weeks back, how the man professed helplessness when his kids were affected.

That same lament nailed Brett now. As he turned toward Wellsville, a poignant Christmas scene called to him from a nearby home. Ground lights bathed stark cutouts, casting a simple silhouette of the Holy Family against a white-washed farmhouse, two anxious parents welcoming a tiny child under austere conditions.

God first.

A wash of faith sweetened its hold on Brett. The

simplistic outline reminded him of who was in control, no matter how much a long-term army guy might think otherwise. So be it. *God, You know me. You've always known me, and You know what a stubborn fool I can be. Heal this boy, Lord. Ease his pain, let him be all right. Help Haley to realize this wasn't her fault, that kids will be kids. And God, just bless us through this. We need You. I need You.*

By the time he got parked and into the E.R., Todd was being evaluated. Haley paced outside the curtained area, frustration and anger darkening her features. He strode toward her, determined to help, wanting to ease her guilt and self-reproach.

Give her time.

An army officer, accustomed to taking command, didn't stand down too well, but in this instance…with the feeling that the Holy Spirit might smack him if he didn't listen…this time he'd offer gentle support and not rugged command. No matter how much it tweaked his take-charge ego. He reached Haley's side, wrapped her in a hug, ignored her resistance and just held her close to his heart until the tears began to fall.

She didn't deserve Brett's help. She didn't deserve these children. Most of all she knew that for all her big talk on following her grandfather's footsteps and building a viable, community-shared business, she could walk away from the entire venture right now and never look back.

The safety of Brett's arms felt good, but knowing she needed that strength just made her weaker, didn't it? Shouldn't she be able to stand on her own two feet?

"Haley?"

She pulled away from Brett and turned quickly.

Katie Bascomb strode toward her, the nurse practitioner from Allegany Family Practice. Her broad smile offered instant reassurance. "Katie, how is he?"

"He's going to be fine." Katie reached out and hugged her before she stepped back and indicated Todd's chart in her hand. "I was here for something else and because our practice is his primary now, they called me down."

"I'm so glad."

"Me, too." Katie motioned for them to sit with her. "Here's what we've got. I want to keep him overnight, but we won't necessarily admit him. We can monitor his sleep right here."

"Is he unconscious?" Haley asked quickly.

"He has a mild concussion, most likely from hitting the pavement when he was knocked down."

Haley fought off the image of this sweet, impetuous boy being mowed down by a huge, monster car.

"The body's natural way of fighting a concussion is to sleep. The brain swelling then reduces itself during that sleep. The impact with the car broke the ulna." She demonstrated the location on her own arm. "That's the thinner forearm bone. The radius was bent and they had to do a reduction on it. That's why you were sent out of the room. He won't remember the procedure, but it's painful for parents to witness."

Parent? She wasn't a parent. She hadn't even been a mediocre aunt.

"I'm giving you a prescription for pain meds. He may or may not need them. I want him to see the orthopedic surgeon on Tuesday for a cast. For the next two days you'll need to keep it immobilized in a sling and a splint. So no wrestling with Tyler."

"What about his breathing?" Haley asked. "The doctor at the co-op said he was breathing shallow."

"Shock," Katie told her. "His body took a blow and the body's reaction is to pause and assess. Shallow breathing is nothing unusual and he's breathing fine now. Has been since they brought him in." She leaned closer and grasped Haley's hand. "He'll be fine. There are no internal injuries other than the concussion and little boys don't generally need to enlist help from cars to get one or two of those as they grow up."

Haley's hint of hope plummeted.

Was this what raising boys was like? What raising children was like? One disaster following another? Katie said the words matter-of-factly, as if this kind of thing happened all the time while parenting. Obviously Haley was cut from a different cloth. Thin. Flimsy. Fairly useless.

Haley swallowed a sigh. "Can we see him?"

"Of course. You guys can stay right here until we release him in the morning. Hang in there, okay?" Katie's gaze said she might be more concerned for

Haley's well being than Todd's, but Haley brushed off the concern with a crisp nod.

"We will."

"He looks so small." Full-grown adults had been wheeled past Haley for the last hour. Seeing Todd in a faded gown, his arm splinted, lying in the hospital bed stabbed her in the gut. He should be home, eating supper, watching TV or wrestling his brother on the floor.

Instead he lay here, a nasty bruised lump marring the left temple, looking way too vulnerable.

Why hadn't she stayed closer to him? Why hadn't she obeyed the instinct to get him home? She knew how impetuous Todd was. And how irascible he got after a drawn-out day.

Brett's phone buzzed. He pulled it out, saw the caller's ID and went to the waiting room to take the call. He returned a few minutes later. His expression said something else was wrong. "What is it? What's happened?"

"Tyler's scared."

"Because his brother almost got killed." Self-loathing surged deeper. "Of course he's scared. He's already lost so much."

"I'm going to go get him," Brett went on.

"Get him?"

"I'll bring him down here so he can see that Todd's going to be fine."

"Here?" The last thing she wanted to do was face Tyler right now. "Tonight?"

"He'll never sleep otherwise. LuAnn says he's beside himself."

Of course he was. He'd known more death, destruction and disruption than any child should be allowed.

Brett leaned down and kissed Todd's cheek. "I'll be right back, buddy."

Haley turned her gaze away, but Brett drew her up. The expression in his eyes showed grave concern, but not for Todd. For her. Because Brett knew she fell down on the job, mixing priorities. Well, she'd set that all straight once the courts reopened for session Monday. She wasn't sure how or when, but one way or another she'd fix this before something worse happened to the boys.

"I'll be right back."

She didn't trust herself to speak. She might say too much, or totally break down. Neither one was an option. He pressed a kiss to her forehead, a sympathetic touch of his lips to her brow. For quick seconds, she was tempted to accept his strength, but she couldn't. Once she revoked her guardianship of those two precious boys, Brett would want nothing more to do with her, and that was to be expected. At this moment, she didn't want all that much to do with herself.

"Haley?" Katie peeked into the room a quarter-hour later. "You're alone?"

Haley nodded. "Brett went to get Tyler. He wants to bring him here and show him that Todd's all right."

"Good idea."

Haley stared at her. "How can it be good for him to see his little brother bruised and broken in a hospital?"

Katie sank into the chair Brett vacated. "Because it's better to see the truth than imagine the worst. Tyler's had a lot going on these past two years."

And Haley had just added to his plate. Sorrow pinched within.

"And my guess is he's got some trust issues," Katie added.

Haley knew the truth of that. "He does."

"So bringing him here to see Todd is the best thing to do. It allays his anxiety and allows him to be the big brother."

The fact that Katie's reasoning made sense made Haley angrier at herself. "How do you and Brett know these things?"

"Well, I—"

Nervous energy pushed Haley up and out of the chair. "You don't have kids. Brett was an absentee father, but you guys all seem to have a handle on this stuff. I'm so totally in over my head, Katie. How can I be trusted to care for these two precious boys if I can't keep them safe?"

"Oh, honey." Katie angled her a matter-of-fact look. "That's the million-dollar question every parent asks themself. And even though I don't have kids, experience has shown me that there are no easy answers in parenting." Katie held her gaze, then inched up her pant leg until a gleaming prosthetic showed. "Accidents happen for a lot of reasons, but look at this." She swept her false leg a good, hard look. "Losing this leg in a car accident was the best thing that happened to me."

Haley frowned, then shook her head. "That makes no sense."

Katie shrugged and dropped the pant leg down. "I made stupid mistakes, but they taught me so much. To love God, to live fresh, to grab all the wonders of life I could because only God knows the day and the hour when we'll be called home."

"You learned all that when?"

Katie laughed softly. "Let's just say the accident started the process. It took a while. But you can't beat yourself up over this. It's unhealthy." She rested her gaze on Todd. "Life comes with risk."

"I don't do risk." Haley had thought otherwise, but she realized tonight that outside of business, she was the most immovable person she knew. At age twenty-eight, how sad was that?

Katie stood and pressed a hand to Haley's shoulder. "Loving comes with risk attached. We risk losing our hearts and our loved ones."

The truth of her words drove Haley's fear deeper.

"But I can't imagine life without loving," Katie continued. "Without caring. Being a Scrooge who sits on the sidelines, guarding funds, letting life pass me by. Risk equates opportunity."

Did it?

Right now Haley couldn't and wouldn't believe it.

"I'll have his discharge papers ready for morning. Once he wakes up we'll send him home. Keep him on the quiet side for a day or two. By the time the cast is put on on Tuesday, he should be ready for normal activity."

Tuesday. If she approached the judge Monday, who would be with her little guy Tuesday? She'd wait, then, until Wednesday. Or Thursday.

A tiny glimmer of how it would feel to walk away from these boys needled her. Was she considering this for their own good? Or hers?

Brett slipped in through the curtains just then. He carried a scared and curious Tyler in one arm. The other held Panther, Todd's well-loved black cat. Without a sound, he plunked the five-year-old into Haley's lap and settled the pajama-clad stuffed animal beneath Todd's good arm as Katie slipped away.

Tyler curled into her. Instinctively her arms went around him, holding him. Nurturing him. How could she stay a step removed while holding a living, breathing little boy whose life turned upside-down so many times already?

Exactly why you should. Aren't you getting this? Are you forgetting the injured child in that bed?

Brett squatted alongside and put a big, broad hand on Tyler's leg. "Todd's sleeping right now. His head got bumped when he hit the ground."

"After the car hit him."

The frank words made Haley's eyes water again.

"Exactly." Brett's voice stayed even. "Todd darted into the parking lot while Aunt Haley was dropping off a key to the cooperative."

"He does that all the time." Tyler squinted up at Brett. "Why doesn't he listen to people?"

"Because he's three."

"Oh." Brett's straightforwardness seemed to make sense to Tyler. He worked his little jaw, then nodded. "I monkeyed around when I was three, too. My mom told me that. She said I climbed everything and that I was lucky to be alive."

Brett's soft smile swept Haley's face. "Sounds like a boy to me."

"So Todd's gonna be all right?"

"Good as new," Brett promised. "And you can be the first person to sign his cast."

"Really?" Concern for his brother disappeared. "I get to be first?"

"Absolutely."

"Sweet!"

Haley couldn't help it. She smiled. And when Brett saw her lips curve, something in his face changed. The worry she'd seen etched there softened. Faded. She couldn't ever remember a time when her smile affected someone like that. It felt…wonderful.

"All right, little man. I've got to get you back home."

"Already?"

"Yes." Brett stood and reached down for Tyler. "You need to sleep so you can help your brother tomorrow.

He's only going to be able to use his left arm, so he might need you to do things for him. And no wrestling for a while."

"Okay. I'll just wrestle with you, then."

"You've got it, partner." He lifted the boy, then dipped him low again. "Give Aunt Haley a kiss goodbye. You'll see her in the morning."

"Bye, Aunt Haley." Tyler's soft lips pressed a kiss to her face while he squeezed her neck with five-year-old vigor. "Love you."

Her heart choked into her throat.

Emotions stirred anew.

Tyler had never said that before. Or even alluded to it. His earnest pledge scared and delighted her.

Brett grazed her cheek with the palm of his hand. He met her gaze with a look of such tenderness that she thought she might break apart inside. "I'll see you tomorrow. I'm going to keep Tyler with me tonight."

"Okay."

His move made perfect sense. In times of crisis, parents would divide and conquer. She may not have experienced that firsthand, but it made great battle strategy, and she was beginning to realize that parenting was kind of like a series of ongoing missions.

No wonder Brett came to it naturally.

Could she get better at it? Did she dare try? She fell asleep in the chair, torn between the safety of self-sacrifice and the loss of two little boys' love.

Chapter Nineteen

Haley stayed home with the boys on Sunday.

On Monday, Tyler went to school. She and Todd sat home and played more games of Memory than should be considered logistically possible.

Tuesday, she took Todd to the orthopedic surgeon for a cast and went home without so much as a stop for fast food.

By Wednesday, she was ready to climb the walls. So was Todd.

Luckily Fiona showed up with baby Reilly Wednesday afternoon. Todd had fallen asleep on the couch, his bruised head and broken arm making him look quite pathetic.

"Oh." Fiona made a face of concern as she saw the little guy's face, his arm. "Oh, Haley, however did you do it?"

Guilt speared. "I didn't mean to, Fee."

Fiona turned, perplexed, then she sputtered, exasperated. "That's not what I meant. I mean, how did you deal with it? I think I'd faint dead away and just add to the problem. I'm a wuss when it comes to this baby."

"That about sums it up."

"Really?" Fiona's face turned hopeful. "You really didn't handle this like you do everything else?"

"Everything else?" Haley frowned, sat down and motioned Fiona to do likewise. "What do you mean?"

"I researched you before I came here," Fee admitted. She set down the baby with an ease she hadn't shown a week before. "And you're amazing. An editor and columnist for the college paper, running an entrepreneurial society, working at the Street of Shops in Lewisburg. And excellent grades."

"And not one of those things prepared me for this." Haley let her gaze rest on the sleeping child. "I don't have a clue what I'm doing and as you can see, I mucked things up already."

Fiona lifted the baby from her seat, crossed the room and deposited her into Haley's arms, ignoring Haley's sputter of protest. "You need to get to know her. She needs to get to know you. Avoiding her won't do you any good."

"You've decided to keep her." Joy nudged some of Haley's guilt aside. "Oh, Fiona, I'm so glad."

"But I'll need help," Fiona told her, flat out. "I'm young and I've made mistakes, but I don't want to make more. Charlie and LuAnn said I can stay there for a while more, but I need to be able to support myself and this baby."

Haley couldn't argue that. "Kids are expensive."

Fee acknowledged that with a pressed-lip nod. "You can say that again. And my mom raised me on public assistance. You know how good our father was at avoiding payments."

Haley's stepfather had made that point repeatedly, that he'd stepped in and paid for what Haley's father created. She'd grown up guilty of her father's malfeasance, the shadows of his misdeeds that helped shut Grandpa's factory down. That pervasive attitude pushed her to fund her own college education. She hit age eighteen determined to go it alone, and she'd done so. But she'd realized these past weeks that being alone wasn't nearly as much fun as she'd pretended.

"Anyway, I've called some of the local shops and put in applications. I can't really start until February, but one way or another, I'm going to take charge of my life. Here. In Jamison. I just wanted to make sure you don't mind if I stay."

"Mind?" Haley frowned at her. "Why would I mind, Fee?"

"Because you didn't expect to have your little sister show up out of the blue, perched on your doorstep, ready to give birth."

True on all counts, but… "I'm glad you're here." She brought Reilly up for a tiny kiss against velvet-soft skin. "And I'm so glad to meet this baby."

"Good." Fee's smile said more than the single word. "Right now I just want to feel like I belong somewhere. Like I'm part of something."

"Like you're wanted."

Fee shrugged. "Yes."

Haley understood perfectly. Reilly started fussing in her arms, and Fee crossed the room, picked her up from Haley, and resettled herself with the nursing cape. "Feeding time."

"You're getting more comfortable." The tiny hint of envy in her tone dismayed Haley.

"Day by day," Fee answered. Once she and the baby were comfortable, she pushed back her brown curls and lifted the opposite shoulder. "But I'm counting on your good example to lead the way. I'm making you my mentor-mother."

Haley snorted. As if. "I can make you a list of mothers who would gladly fit the bill. And not one of them would be me."

"Then we'll learn together," Fee decided. "That's what sisters are for, right?"

It was, Haley realized. But how could she willingly agree to keep the boys long-term if she couldn't manage to keep them safe?

Brett called just then.

She let the call go to voice mail. He'd stopped by with food, with DVDs and coloring books, with gentle words of wisdom.

She'd avoided all of it, afraid he'd hate her if she let the boys go and that she'd hate herself if anything else happened to them.

A text alert appeared. Brett never texted her. But when she opened the text, she saw why he hadn't resorted to voice mail. Voice mail she could ignore. His text?

No way.

Taking Todd tomorrow while Tyler's in school. Sit home or go to work. Your choice.

Haley's mouth dropped open.

"Trouble?" Fee asked. She shifted her left brow up in question.

"Trouble for Brett Stanton if he thinks he can boss me around," Haley sputtered.

Fee dipped her chin, smiling.

"It's not funny."

Fee shook her head, eyes down, but Haley was pretty sure her lips still quirked up. "Of course not. How awful to have a marvelous, gorgeous man willing to help you out. Take care of you. Help with the kids. I don't know a woman on Earth who'd like that."

"Very funny."

Fee slanted the smile Haley's way as she finished nursing the baby. "Look me in the eye and tell me you're not over-the-moon in love with the guy and just too afraid of following our parents' foolish footprints."

In love with the guy.

In love with Brett.

His warmth. His solidity. His breadth of spirit and broad-chested vigor. The strength of a soldier in a spiritual man. A man whose very presence made her long to draw closer. Seek more time. Not once had he blamed her for Todd's accident, but a battle-ready, decorated army veteran like Brett must recoil from the weakness within her. Wouldn't he?

"I think you might be overthinking things," Fee observed as she stood to pack up a now-sleeping Reilly. "And I might be young and foolish, and I might be guilty of loving the wrong guy—" her gaze shifted to the peaceful baby in her arms "—but I still believe in the fairy tale. The happily ever afters. But from now on, I'm going to let faith and common sense guide me. Because now I have so much more riding on it."

The look she settled on the sleeping newborn made Haley realize they weren't all that different. Both searching, both needing, despite their age difference.

She cooked fried bologna for dinner and felt like a Food Network diva for making the boys so happy. By the time she got them into bed, she was exhausted mentally and psyched physically.

She sank onto the couch and surveyed the festive room. Her gaze rested on the Nativity scene. Two wooly sheep had been uprooted from their rightful spots. She picked them up off the carpet and gently set them in place. Her hand lingered as she studied the pieces.

Joseph, big and strong, a carpenter. Older than Mary, maybe wiser? Mary, heartfelt and trusting, but she had to be afraid, hadn't she? And wasn't her fear tested numerous times when those in power threatened her child?

Fee's expression came back to her, the look of a mother determined to make her way for her baby.

Mary had been young. So young. But she'd taken charge despite her qualms, facing possible scorn and punishment for being an unwed mother, letting her faith uplift her. "My soul glorifies the Lord, and my spirit rejoices in God, my savior…" Her sweet, simple prayer, the magnificat, a song of acceptance.

And Joseph stood by her, taking stand on a quiet promise in the night, an angel's word. How could she do less for these boys?

Man up.

Anthony had used that expression the few times she met him. She regretted not getting to know him better, but maybe God had given her a chance to do that now, by raising her brother's sons.

And Fee was here, her sister, a pretty young woman in search of family, just like Haley. She stood, stretched and peeked in at the boys, tumbled in sleep. Tyler, just beginning to move beyond the shadows and fears that dogged him. Todd, a bit broken but healing from his impetuous act. She and he had both learned a hard lesson that day.

She glanced back at the manger scene, a tiny depiction of a most holy night. Could she do this?

Yes. She was silly and scared to think otherwise.

Should she do it? Care for two little boys who needed so much love, so much time that she might end up frazzled at the end of the day?

Of course she should. What mother wasn't frazzled

by the busyness of life? She'd just have to find a balance between busy and crazy, but she thought of the women around her. Maude, an active grandmother running a business. LuAnn, a woman who'd raised her kids and others' children, giving, laughing, sharing every day of her life. Tina, a stalwart soul, tough and in charge, always willing to make things better.

She wanted to be like them. A take-charge woman who finds that balance of faith, hope and love. From this moment forward, she was determined to do just that.

Chapter Twenty

Brett strode up Haley's steps, resolved to have his say. No matter how much Haley hemmed and hawed, he was taking a stance. Todd was getting out of this house and seeing the world today, no matter how nervous it made her.

The door whipped open before he had a chance to knock. "Here you go." Haley flashed him a quick smile as she propelled the three-year-old forward. "He's very excited to be spending the day with you."

A happy grin brightened Todd's face. The new camouflage jacket Brett bought him fit over the cast loosely, and left plenty of room to grow into next year. A camo hat and mittens completed the mini-soldier look.

Brett reached down and scooped the little man up, then planted a kiss on his cheek.

"That tickles!" Todd giggled out loud as Brett nuzzled in.

"Hey, I shaved."

He went perfectly still when Haley's soft hand tested his cheek for nubbiness. The feel of her fingers, cool and slim, the fruit-salad scent of her lotion softened by a hint of vanilla…

She flashed him a grin, tapped his cheek lightly and said, "I think you need a new blade, big guy. Kinda rough for first thing in the morning, isn't it?"

He caught her hand. Held it. Then let his tone say more than his words. "Is it?"

She paused, her gaze locked on her hand in his, then she sighed, soft and low, the kind of sound that made him yearn for the dream he thought he'd missed years ago. "No."

Her whispered answer made him grin and want to conquer vast worlds. But for today, he'd just take the kid off her hands and let her get to work. "I'll bring him and Tyler home tonight. We've got a project going with my mom and this guy's accident put us behind. So we're finishing things up after school and that way you can work until closing."

"What if I don't want to?"

"How's that?" Brett turned, puzzled.

"What if I don't want to spend twelve hours working?" Haley asked. "What if I want to spend the evening with you guys?"

He leaned down, cupped the back of her head with his free hand and kissed her. "Music to my ears. We'll meet at my place for supper. Five-thirty."

She nodded, stepped outside and locked the door behind her. "See you then."

He tucked Todd into his car seat while Haley walked around the corner to the cooperative's entrance. Her green peacoat and mottled Christmas scarf looked great on her, contrasted against the snow.

"Brett! Can we go now?"

Brett pulled his gaze away from Haley and nodded. "Yes, buddy. Yes, we can."

"Haley Jennings?"

Haley turned from the display she was fixing and smiled right off, then stuck out her hand. "Mrs. Stanton."

"Joanna, yes." Brett's mother looked puzzled. "How did you know?"

"Brett looks like you. Only bigger."

Pleasure lighted the older woman's gaze. She took Haley's hand and Haley sensed a quiver of nervousness. "Would you like some coffee, Joanna? Or tea? Soda?" She indicated the retro diner with a thrust of her chin. "My treat."

Joanna shook her head. "I don't have a lot of time, but I was over this way with my friend and…" She hesitated, prissed her lips, then breathed out. "Do you mind if I spend time with your boys?"

This wasn't the spin Haley expected. She frowned, puzzled. "No. Why?"

"I'm an alcoholic."

Understanding dawned. Haley nodded. "Brett told me."

Joanna's expression showed no surprise. "My son

is a full disclosure kind of guy. And that's not a bad thing," she added. She drew a breath, gazed around, then brought her eyes back to Haley. "I wasn't a good mother."

Haley made a sympathetic noise of understanding.

"I can admit that, although I'm ashamed of myself. But I've got all the time the good Lord gives me now, and I just wanted you to know that I like spending time with those little boys. It's as if—" she faltered again, then waded in "—as if God's giving me a second chance to do things right. But I didn't want you to worry about them when I'm around. I thought it was better if I just came to talk to you directly."

Brave, thought Haley. A quality this woman passed on to her son. "You've made the decision not to drink anymore?"

"I have." Joanna's firm tone matched the clarity of her eyes.

"Then I think it's wonderful for the boys to have you around," Haley told her honestly. "Brett says you're very creative."

"That's nice of him to say. I try to be."

"And that you don't mind noise."

Joanna smiled. "Not in the least."

"Well, then." Haley hoped her matching smile offered reassurance. "Because I'm finding my way step by step with this new role, I'm more than happy to have company. Welcome aboard, Joanna. You sure you wouldn't like coffee or something? It will take only a few minutes and I could use a break."

"Well." Joanna glanced around, then acquiesced. "My friend Sue is shopping and that may take a while, so, sure." She straightened her shoulders and moved with Haley toward the café. "A cup of coffee sounds real good right about now."

"Can we give them to her now, Brett? Puuuhleeeease?"

Haley shed her jacket, tossed it on the back of a chair alongside Brett's entry and sent a mischievous frown Todd's way a little after five that night. "Do you have a secret, little man?"

"For Christmas," Brett scolded. He took her jacket from the back of the chair and hung it on its rightful hook, alongside the boys' coats. "No peeking."

"It's almost Christmas," Haley argued. "And girls love presents."

"Do they?" Brett's smile said that wasn't exactly a revelation.

"Everybody loves presents." Tyler sidled up next to Haley. He looked suddenly uncomfortable and wriggled. His brow creased.

"Are you okay, Ty?" Brett set plates on the table for Haley to spread around.

Tyler shrugged one shoulder. Concern wrinkled his brow. "Shouldn't we go see Santa Claus soon? Or send him a letter? Because Christmas is really, really close, right?"

His worried gaze said he'd been thinking about this

a long, long time. Possibly a day or two. Haley turned toward Brett. "Tonight?"

He had the grace not to look surprised that she was willing to jump in, both feet. He scanned the clock, then turned the burners off. "Get your coats, boys."

"Really?"

"Really!"

"We can save the burgers for tomorrow, the roads are clear and it's early enough. Let's go."

"I can't believe it." Todd drew out the *l* carefully, practicing. "I'm going to see Santa Claus. I'll give him the biggest hug ever."

"Me, too."

Tyler's declaration made Haley's night. Such a little thing, to take time to go see Santa on the spur of the moment, but meaningful to a child. And Tyler wasn't free with his hugs, like Todd, so to offer one to Santa? That highlighted the little boy's longing. "Of course we won't ask for too much," she reminded them as they moved to the car. "It's never good to be greedy."

"I've got a few things to check out with the old fellow myself," said Brett as he eased the car onto the road. "We'll just see if he comes through."

"Of course he will." Haley turned and met his teasing look with one of her own. "Because it's Christmas, Brett."

By the time they visited Santa and grabbed a quick supper, bedtime loomed.

"They're zonked." Haley closed the door with a

quiet click and sank onto the couch, hoping Brett might join her.

He did. Then he lifted her hand, pressed a kiss to the palm and held it gently against the rough of his cheek. "Thank you for tonight."

"It was fun, wasn't it?"

He leaned back, put an arm around her shoulders and drew her close. "The best."

"Do you think your mom can keep the boys Friday night so we can Christmas shop together?"

"You're okay with that?" He leaned around to see her face. "Really?"

"I think she's trying hard and deserves our trust," Haley answered.

Brett couldn't disagree. "I was wondering…"

"Yes?" She drew the word out to match his stretched-out tone.

"If we could have Christmas together. All of us. Like a family."

She turned in his arm and her smile said he didn't need words, but the words only compounded his happiness. "I think that would be perfect. You, me, the boys, your mother, Fiona and the baby and Charlie and LuAnn because Jess's family is going to her in-laws on Christmas Day."

"You've already planned it?"

"Hoped," she corrected. She leaned up and planted a kiss to his chin, a kiss that found its way to his mouth when she smiled. "I hoped for just that and now we'll plan it together."

He'd been doing some planning of his own the past few days, determined to grab life anew. Planning a Christmas celebration with Haley made it seem even more possible.

Chapter Twenty-One

Brett figured they made an interesting crew at Christmas morning services. Todd and Tyler, excited and anxious to get on with their day and open presents. His mother, looking very much the grandmother as she doled out fruit snacks to one, then the other, buying time and quiet. Charlie and LuAnn, pleased to be part of a big family again. Fiona, holding Reilly, the tiny girl dressed in a My First Christmas red-and-white sleeper.

And Haley, a red plaid Christmas ribbon clipping the top of her long braid. The sight of her and those boys, dressed for a holiday with him made his heart soar.

Yes, it was soon.

Yes, they had time.

But he'd spent over twenty years on the sidelines. Now he wanted to be in the game, fully immersed. He only hoped and prayed she wanted the same thing.

Once church was over, Brett commandeered Haley

and the boys. When he headed east out of town, she turned, confused. "Do we have a stop to make?"

The boys watched, intrigued, but not complaining even though gifts awaited them back at Haley's. "A quick stop out here."

"On Christmas?" She wrinkled her nose. "Brett, nothing's open on Christmas, is it?"

"No."

She frowned, then shifted her attention to the boys. "Hey, you two. Do you know what's going on?"

"No." Tyler shook his head but couldn't quite hide the gleam in his eye.

"I don't know anything, eiver!" Todd declared, but Haley's look said she wasn't buying it. Just before she opened her mouth to wrangle information out of Todd, Brett pulled up Buehrings Road and parked in front of the horse barn.

The boys giggled and scrambled out of their seats.

"We're getting out?"

"Yes."

"Brett, it's Christmas," she scolded as she climbed out of the SUV. "It's winter, it's cold, I'm in church clothes and we have people waiting for us."

"LuAnn and my mother have it covered," he promised.

"They knew we weren't coming straight back?"

"Let's just say they suspected as much."

Haley drew a deep breath. She didn't know a whole lot about throwing a family shindig, but she did know it was appropriate to show up, and she was about to remind Brett of that when the big, broad-chested soldier went down on one knee.

Her heart clutched.

Her hands clenched.

Her chin quivered as she thought of just how amazing this man was.

"I fink she's happy," Todd whispered loudly.

Tyler squirmed, but he looked pretty happy himself.

"Haley Jennings, I know we haven't known each other long, and I—"

"Yes."

He stared at her, hard. "You didn't let me finish."

She dimpled. "Do you really need to? I think my answer summed it all up."

"A man would still like the opportunity to actually pose the question."

"Oh. Well, in that case." She dropped a wink to the boys. "Pose away, Colonel."

He smiled up at her, and in that smile she saw the grace and goodness of a man like no other she'd ever known.

"Haley Jennings, would you do me the honor of marrying a crusty old soldier like me and letting me be a father to these two little boys? In the interest of everyone's health, it might behoove you to know that it's very cold down here in the snow."

"Oh, you silly, delightful man." She reached down, pulled him up and laughed when he twirled her around in the snow. "Yes, yes and yes. I will be delighted to marry you and raise these two beautiful boys together."

"Leaving ourselves open to the possibility that they may at some point be joined by younger brothers and sisters?"

"At some point." She sent him a look that said one step at a time. "And I wouldn't object to a little girl with her daddy's hazel eyes and my naturally curly hair."

That made him grin.

The boys swooped in, offering their approval. "We get to live with the trains," Tyler whooped.

"And Derringer will be my doggie," Todd added.

"*Our* doggie."

"I love him more than you do."

"Do not."

"Do so."

"Do—"

"And on that note." Brett scooped Todd up, leaned down and gave Haley a sweet, long kiss, a kiss that held the joy of the moment and the promise of tomorrow. "I've got one more question to ask."

Haley snuggled in with the boys, the feel of Brett's arms, his strength and warmth, wonderful beyond words. "What's that?"

"I'd like to buy this barn, this land. We can have the barn made over into a house…"

"With so much room to run," shouted Tyler. He

wriggled free and jumped into the air. "I would love to live out here with Derringer, Aunt Haley! Please say yes!"

For the first time in a long, busy month, Tyler was acting like an excited, normal little boy. A child of hope, his fears erased, at least for the moment. That blessing, that step forward…

She reached up and drew Brett down for one last kiss. "I'd love that, Brett. So much. And I bet your mom would be a good one to help me plan things out. The minute I saw those Christmas ornaments, I knew she and I would see eye-to-eye."

Her words pleased him. She saw it in his smile, his eyes.

Todd tugged his sleeve.

Brett leaned down. "Do you have to use the bathroom?"

Todd made a face at him. "No. You forgot the ring."

"Got it right here," Brett assured him. He pulled out a navy velvet jewelry box and flipped open the lid. A sapphire-and-diamond ring gleamed against the satin setting. "Do you like it?" he wondered as he slipped it out of the box. "I wanted something as pretty as your eyes, but this was as close as I could get."

"Oh, Brett." She threw her arms around him and hugged him, then stood back and let him place the ring on her finger. "I don't like it. I *love* it."

His smile said she'd used the perfect words. He bent, brushed a quick kiss to her mouth, then herded Todd over to his side of the car. Tyler climbed up into his seat, his smile marking the day.

And that little-boy grin was the best Christmas present Haley could have imagined.

Epilogue

"Do you have Todd?" Brett wondered, glancing around the driveway late Easter morning.

"No. I thought you had him."

Brett made a face. "Oops."

Haley cupped her hands around her mouth, yelled for Todd, then sent a bemused look to Brett as the little boy came racing over from the convenience store. "Nipping cookies, I bet."

"Growing boy." Brett laughed as he caught the boy up and noogied his head. "We're having dinner with Grandma. Stop eating."

"I'm so hungry." Todd breathed the words through a mouthful of sugar cookie. Crumbs spattered Brett's clean white shirt. Haley brushed them away once they had Todd belted in his seat, and Brett seized the moment for a quick kiss and a smile.

Oh, that smile.

"We're good?"

"Flowers, dessert, two boys dressed in camouflage."

She hiked a brow at that, then sighed. "I don't know what was wrong with your Easter suits, boys."

"This is cooler." Tyler pulled his camo cap low on his brow. "Now we look like Dad in the army."

"And Brett," Todd added.

"You look adorable," Haley assured them.

Both boys scowled.

"She means rugged, boys." Brett met their gazes through the rearview mirror. "Fierce."

"Yeah!"

"Yeah."

"I am so in over my head," Haley murmured.

His big right hand covered her left one. "There's two of us. Man-to-man defense. We've got it covered." He angled the car up the driveway of the well-treed cemetery in Bolivar a short while later. He steered the SUV around the winding road, then pulled to a stop just short of a wooded hillside. While Haley gathered the boys, Brett retrieved a patriotic wreath from the back of the SUV.

"Ready?" Haley sent him a look of encouragement and faith. True faith.

He nodded. "Yes. Finally."

She slipped her hand into his free one and they climbed the small hill together.

Josiah's name lay centered in gray granite. The dates showed a life cut short, but as Brett positioned the arrangement with care, his face didn't look tormented. Shaded, yes. But when he stood and they all locked hands, Brett's words bathed Haley's heart and soul.

"Lord, You blessed me with a son once." He paused, the warmth of a mid-April Easter teasing early songbirds to rejoice. "And now again." He smiled down at the two little boys flanking them. Todd reached up and Brett obliged him by picking him up, holding the boy alongside his chest. "I'd just like to say thank You for both opportunities."

He saluted the grave.

Solemn, the boys followed suit.

Haley blinked back tears and slipped an arm around Tyler's shoulders. "Your turn."

Brett set Todd down. The boys moved forward and put the small American flag in place, then they stopped, saluted their big brother and stepped back.

Brett cleared his throat. Seconds passed. Then he crouched low, hugged both boys and stood, one in each arm. "I think it's time we went to Grandma's for dinner."

"I'm starving."

"Me, too."

"Why can't Derringer come?"

"Because—"

"I told you why."

"Well, I can't have Easter without my dog."

"Hush, both of you." Brett's tone quieted the boys. He set them down alongside the car and bent low again. "We'll bring Derringer some ham," he promised Todd. Then he turned Tyler's way. "And you remind me of another bossy big brother I knew a long time ago."

"Really?" Tyler lit up, intrigued. "Who?"

Brett sighed and motioned for him to get into the car. "Me," he admitted. He sent Haley a quick smile and a wink as the boys squabbled, racing to get their buckles fastened. "Have I mentioned today how much I love you? And this." He waved a hand toward the noisy boys, and the smile he sent her…

That sweet, crooked smile…

Made her feel like she could handle anything life sent her. "Never often enough," she declared as she climbed into the car and sneaked a quick kiss. "But I'll be delighted to spend a lifetime hearing it."

"Me, too."

* * * * *

If you enjoyed Ruth Logan Herne's story,
be sure to check out the other books this month
from Love Inspired!

Dear Reader,

On Memorial Day in 2010 I stood alongside a tall, strong forty-something soldier. I didn't know him. He didn't know me. He watched that small home-town parade with grave intent. On the back side of his military cap were tiny yellow ribbons, marking two memories in a quiet, private way.

I knew I had to write a story about him. Whoever he was. That stoic soldier became the basis for Colonel Brett Stanton, retired, U.S. Army. And those two ribbons became symbols for Ben and Josiah. Most of us are honored when others emulate us, but when that example leads loved ones to an early grave, the resulting guilt weighs heavy, especially at holiday time.

God doesn't want us to live life with heavy hearts. We are sons and daughters of the King and He wants us happy…but He does expect us to do our best each day. Putting a young woman like Haley in Brett's path made perfect sense. She's longed for the stability of a mature man, a man of deep appreciation. A man of faith and hope, the kind who stays the course. And a ready-made family? Isn't that the best gift of Christmas, a child? In this book we have two beautiful boys in need of a stable, normal home. A chance to be someone's beloved child again.

I hope you enjoy reading their story, a tale of faith, hope and love. And homemade chicken and biscuits is never a bad thing! Feel free to email me at ruthy@

ruthloganherne.com, visit me at themenofallegany-county.blogspot.com or my website www.ruthlogan-herne.com or write to me care of Love Inspired Books, 233 Broadway, Suite 1001, New York, NY 10279.

God bless you and Merry Christmas!
Ruthy

Questions for Discussion

1. Haley is en route to a whole new chapter of her life because she's taking charge of her brother's orphaned boys, Tyler and Todd. Have you ever had a sharp bend in the road like that? What was it and how did you handle it?

2. The Jamison Hose Company is giving up their private holiday celebrations to feed the hungry. Does your town or city sponsor events like this? Have you ever volunteered to staff them? How did that experience work out for you?

3. Haley is touched by the gentle outreach that surrounds her at the holiday feast. The older folks are invigorated by her arrival with two little boys. Why are older folks often drawn to small children these days?

4. Brett is immediately drawn to the young woman and the boys. They remind him of his brother and his son, both lost at war. Has God ever put people in your path to help you clear emotional hurdles?

5. Brett's holiday weekend is turned upside down when his presence is required at the Crossroads Mini-Mart. Being thrust into a hands-on position revitalizes him. And when he's able to help Haley feed the boys dinner, another barrier breaks down.

He feels needed and appreciated. Has God ever amazed you with multiple circumstances that work together to help you?

6. When Brett and Haley meet at church, she realizes she's smitten, but now she's doubly cautious because she's suddenly responsible for two busy, boisterous boys. How difficult would it be for a childless person to suddenly take on the care of two preschoolers?

7. The grand opening of Bennington Station has Haley running morning, noon and night. But the boys need care. Guilt grows. How hard is it for parents to find a proper balance of work to play? How important is it to learn to delegate and accept help?

8. Brett's mother has had ups and downs with alcoholism, but meeting the little boys seems to give her new hope. Do you know people who have overcome substance abuse? Has it been an upward struggle for them, too?

9. Haley's promise of a nice, normal Christmas doesn't seem close to coming true because of the demands on her time. Have you often meant for things to go one way, only to have life push them in the opposite direction? How do you handle that?

10. Haley's guilt over the accident is understandable, but it's compounded by her lack of experience with children. How difficult would it be to suddenly be responsible for the livelihood of over forty families and two little boys who didn't know your name a few weeks ago?

11. Brett wishes he'd been a better father to Josiah. He's surprised that Josiah's mother sees things very differently. Have you ever run into that, where another person's assessment is the opposite of your own? Have you ever gotten a wake-up call simply through someone else's commonsense point of view?

12. Haley longs for family stability. Brett would love a second chance to be a better father. Fiona would like to make better choices and be loved and accepted. Was it chance or God's loving plan that brought them all together for a beautiful family-filled Christmas?

LARGER-PRINT BOOKS!

GET 2 FREE
LARGER-PRINT NOVELS
PLUS 2 FREE
MYSTERY GIFTS

Love Inspired

Larger-print novels are now available...

YES! Please send me 2 FREE LARGER-PRINT Love Inspired® novels and my 2 FREE mystery gifts (gifts are worth about $10). After receiving them, if I don't wish to receive any more books, I can return the shipping statement marked "cancel". If I don't cancel, I will receive 6 brand-new novels every month and be billed just $4.99 per book in the U.S. or $5.49 per book in Canada. That's a saving of at least 23% off the cover price. It's quite a bargain! Shipping and handling is just 50¢ per book in the U.S. and 75¢ per book in Canada.* I understand that accepting the 2 free books and gifts places me under no obligation to buy anything. I can always return a shipment and cancel at any time. Even if I never buy another book, the two free books and gifts are mine to keep forever.

122/322 IDN FEG3

Name _____ (PLEASE PRINT) _____

Address _____ Apt. #

City _____ State/Prov. _____ Zip/Postal Code

Signature (if under 18, a parent or guardian must sign)

Mail to the **Reader Service**:
IN U.S.A.: P.O. Box 1867, Buffalo, NY 14240-1867
IN CANADA: P.O. Box 609, Fort Erie, Ontario L2A 5X3

Not valid to current subscribers to Love Inspired Larger-Print books.

**Are you a current subscriber to Love Inspired books
and want to receive the larger-print edition?
Call 1-800-873-8635 or visit www.ReaderService.com.**

* Terms and prices subject to change without notice. Prices do not include applicable taxes. Sales tax applicable in N.Y. Canadian residents will be charged applicable taxes. Offer not valid in Quebec. This offer is limited to one order per household. All orders subject to credit approval. Credit or debit balances in a customer's account(s) may be offset by any other outstanding balance owed by or to the customer. Please allow 4 to 6 weeks for delivery. Offer available while quantities last.

Your Privacy—The Reader Service is committed to protecting your privacy. Our Privacy Policy is available online at www.ReaderService.com or upon request from the Reader Service.

We make a portion of our mailing list available to reputable third parties that offer products we believe may interest you. If you prefer that we not exchange your name with third parties, or if you wish to clarify or modify your communication preferences, please visit us at www.ReaderService.com/consumerchoice or write to us at Reader Service Preference Service, P.O. Box 9062, Buffalo, NY 14269. Include your complete name and address.

LILP11B

Love Inspired®
SUSPENSE
RIVETING INSPIRATIONAL ROMANCE

Watch for our series of edge-
of-your-seat suspense novels.
These contemporary tales
of intrigue and romance
feature Christian characters
facing challenges to their faith...
and their lives!

**AVAILABLE IN REGULAR
& LARGER-PRINT FORMATS**

FAMOUS FAMILIES

YES! Please send me the *Famous Families* collection featuring the Fortunes, the Bravos, the McCabes and the Cavanaughs. This collection will begin with 3 FREE BOOKS and 2 FREE GIFTS in my very first shipment— and more valuable free gifts will follow! My books will arrive in 8 monthly shipments until I have the entire 51-book *Famous Families* collection. I will receive 2-3 free books in each shipment and I will pay just $4.49 U.S./$5.39 CDN for each of the other 4 books in each shipment, plus $2.99 for shipping and handling.* If I decide to keep the entire collection, I'll only have paid for 32 books because 19 books are free. I understand that accepting the 3 free books and gifts places me under no obligation to buy anything. I can always return a shipment and cancel at any time. My free books and gifts are mine to keep no matter what I decide.

268 HCN 0387   468 HCN 0387

Name	(PLEASE PRINT)	
Address		Apt. #
City	State/Prov.	Zip/Postal Code

Signature (if under 18, a parent or guardian must sign)

Mail to the **Reader Service:**

IN U.S.A.: P.O. Box 1867, Buffalo, NY 14240-1867
IN CANADA: P.O. Box 609, Fort Erie, Ontario L2A 5X3

* Terms and prices subject to change without notice. Prices do not include applicable taxes. Sales tax applicable in N.Y. Canadian residents will be charged applicable taxes. This offer is limited to one order per household. All orders subject to approval. Credit or debit balances in a customer's account(s) may be offset by any other outstanding balance owed by or to the customer. Please allow 4 to 6 weeks for delivery. Offer available while quantities last. Offer not available to Quebec residents.

FFBPA12

Reader Service.com

Manage your account online!
- Review your order history
- Manage your payments
- Update your address

We've designed the Reader Service website just for you.

Enjoy all the features!
- Reader excerpts from any series
- Respond to mailings and special monthly offers
- Discover new series available to you
- Browse the Bonus Bucks catalogue
- Share your feedback

Visit us at:

ReaderService.com

RS12